UNTIL DELILAH
A HAPPILY EVER ALPHA NOVEL

HARLOW LAYNE

Until Delilah by Harlow Layne

Copyright © 2021 by Harlow Layne

ALL RIGHTS RESERVED

Published by Boom Factory Publishing, LLC.

Harlow Layne CONTRIBUTOR to the Original Works was granted permission by Aurora Rose Reynolds, ORIGINAL AUTHOR, to use the copyrighted characters and / or worlds created by Aurora Rose Reynolds in the Original Work; all copyright protection to the characters and / or worlds of Aurora Rose Reynolds in the Original Works are and shall continue to be retained by Aurora Rose Reynolds. You can find all of Aurora Rose Reynolds Original Works on most major retailers. No part of this publication may be reproduced, transmitted, downloaded, distributed, stored in or introduced into any information storage or retrieval system, in any form or by any means, whether electronic, photocopying, mechanical or otherwise, without express permission of the publisher, except by a reviewer who may quote brief passages for review purposes. This book is a work of fiction. Names, characters, places, story lines and incidents are the product of the author's imagination or are used fictitiously. Any resemblances to actual persons, living or dead, events, locales or any events or occurrences are purely coincidental.

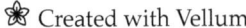 Created with Vellum

UNTIL DELILAH

Join Harlow's mailing list to be the first to know of new releases, free books, sales, and other giveaways!

https://harlowlayne.com/newsletter/

Something about Delilah draws me in from the first moment we meet. The fact that she's a single mom, to the sweetest kid ever, is just a bonus.

I've got my work cut out for me when it comes to showing her what real love is— first I'll have to earn her trust and prove I'm not going anywhere.

After seeing her fading bruises and split lip, my protective instincts kick in and I know I would do anything to keep them safe. But she keeps pushing me away, afraid her secrets will put me in danger.

My whole life I've grown up hearing about the boom. I wasn't sure my time would come… Until Delilah.

Until Delilah is part of Aurora Rose Reynolds's Happily Ever Alpha World. If you loved Until December, then you'll want to read Until Delilah.

PROLOGUE
DELILAH

HOLDING MY BREATH, I slide out of bed trying not to jostle the mattress or the man sleeping next to me. Once my feet hit the floor, I use every muscle in my body to stand without shaking the bed. I look over my shoulder and let out a silent sigh of relief before I slowly bring up the Uber app, praying the light from my phone doesn't wake him, and order a ride. Once I see it's confirmed, I turn off my phone and shove it underneath the mattress as far as I can, all the while trying to keep from waking Bradley.

Tip toeing into the closet, I retrieve the bag I packed earlier in the day after I got home from the hospital, and sling it over my shoulder.

Walking backward, I count my steps; ten, nine, eight and so on while I keep an eye on the sleeping figure. When I hit one, I turn on my heel and walk as quickly as I can while still being silent. When Beckham's door comes into view, I slip inside his room, but leave the door open a crack so I can hear any noises coming from the hall. I give myself one moment to stare down at my son and pray with all that's holy that it won't be too long before he'll be sleeping as peacefully as he is in this moment.

Wiping a tear that's slowly trailing down my cheek, I lean down and pick my son up, hoping he'll sleep through everything, but I don't get my wish. His toe head pops up and his sleepy blue eyes try to focus on me.

"Mama, what's going on?" he asks, voice clogged with sleep.

Placing a finger over his mouth to quiet him, I start to leave his room, but then remember the polar bear my parents got him when they went to Antarctica two years ago. He hasn't slept without it since they gave it to him.

Circling back to his bed, I pick Chewy up and shove him between Beck and me since he's already fallen back asleep. I can't risk Beckham's heartbreak if Chewy is dropped and left behind.

Headlights flash through his bedroom window, making my heart race double time. I'm scared of what lies ahead for our future, but I know this is what I need to do to keep us safe.

In my head, I count the stairs as I descend to the living room, making sure I don't step on the one squeaky stair that will alert my departure. I never understood why Bradley wouldn't fix it, but now I wonder if it was in case of this very scenario. I know if I get caught now, it's likely Bradley will kill me, Beckham, and my unborn baby.

After turning off the alarm, I open the front door, but stop when it lets out a loud noise that I swear could wake the dead and very well might have woken my boyfriend.

No, not my boyfriend.

My ex-boyfriend.

He just doesn't know it yet. He won't know until he wakes up in the morning and finds us gone.

Holding onto Beckham with everything in me, I run out of the house and down the sidewalk to the waiting car. I don't even sit Beckham down in the seat before I slide in and buckle us both in with him on my lap.

"Go," I urge the driver as sweat starts to form along my hairline.

The man turns in his seat, his brows furrow as he looks me up and down. "Is everything okay, ma'am?"

"It will be if you drive. Now," I whisper yell. Locking eyes on him, I beg. "Please."

He doesn't say a word as he turns around and looks up at the stately house. I swear I see Bradley at the window and my heart nearly stops dead in my chest.

Leaning forward with my hands on the headrest in front of me, I plead with the driver to drive before I have a nervous breakdown in his back seat or have a heart attack from stress.

The driver doesn't speak as he takes the car out of park

and slowly starts to reverse down the driveway. Once we've been on the road for a few minutes, his soft voice breaks the silence. "Are you and your boy okay?"

"We are now thanks to you." I lean my head back and close my eyes. For the last twenty-four hours, I've lived in fear since I found out my boyfriend is involved in some very illegal shit. Now I can finally take a deep breath.

"Wasn't that the Stanton residence?"

My right eye cracks open so I can take in the man driving. Is he one of their goons and he's going to take me back? "It was," I answer hesitantly.

"I never liked those Stanton's. They think they're better than everyone else when really they're the scum beneath all of our shoes."

"I couldn't agree more, but don't let anyone hear you say that. You never know who's on their side." I pray I'm not making a mistake by saying those words.

"If I'm asked, I'll say you asked to be dropped off somewhere else along the way. I've already logged off, so they won't be able to see if I took you to the bus station or not."

How had I not thought of that? If this good man hadn't logged off, Bradley would have been able to track me to the bus station and then likely to where I bought tickets as well. At least I bought tickets to multiple places, so he'll have to try and track me down at all of them, and I know Bradley won't rest until he eventually finds me.

A few minutes later we pull up outside the bus station.

The driver doesn't turn around and wish me luck. He sits looking straight ahead as if this is any other trip for him.

The sound of my seatbelt unclipping and opening the car door makes everything real. I'm free. At least for now.

Almost as if on instinct, Beckham's arms tighten around me, but that's the only sign he gives me he's even remotely awake.

Bending down so I can see inside the car, I make eye contact with the driver through the rearview mirror. "Thank you. You have no idea how much you're helping me and my son."

The driver's only response is to nod before I close the door and he drives off.

Looking around, I see there's no one around, which is exactly why I picked this time of night to arrive. It will give me just enough time to do what I need to do before our bus departs.

My eyes dart around the area as I make my way inside the public restroom. Luckily, there's a long counter for me to sit Beckham down on. His tired eyes crack open and then squint in the harsh light.

Brushing the blond hair off his forehead, I hug my little boy who shouldn't have to pay for the mistakes I've made. "I know you're tired, sweet boy, but you've got to stay awake for a little while, and then you can sleep for as long as you want."

His little hands wrap around my waist and hug me back. "What are we doing?"

"We're going to go on a long bus ride and then we're going to start a new life away from Bradley. Would you like that?"

Beckham pulls back to look up at me. "He's scary, Mama. I don't want him to ever hurt you again." His finger comes up and almost touches my black, swollen eye, but stops at the last second.

"Me either baby, that's why we're leaving. We're going to find someplace safe to live, but first I need to color my hair."

"But why, Mama?" he asks innocently.

"So, no one will recognize me." I pull out his favorite Yankee's baseball hat and place it on top of his head, hiding his nearly white hair. I don't want to color his hair if I don't have to. I'm not sure how good it is for someone so young to have their hair colored.

"I'll know who you are." He smiles.

"Yes, you will. You'll be the only one. It will be our little secret. Would you like to help me mix the color?" I open the box and let him pull out all the bottles and creams. After reading the instructions, I hold up one of the tiny bottles and ask. "Do you want to pour this in the big bottle?"

He nods and gets to work. While he's trying not to spill any of the liquid, I pull out a pair of kitchen scissors and cut my hair that reaches the middle of my back until it sits above my shoulders. My hair has been long for as long as I can remember, and no one would suspect I'd cut and color it. It's painful to cut it, but I know it needs to be done to keep us safe.

"Now shake it up as hard as you can," I instruct as I put on the pair of latex gloves the box provided.

"Are you coloring your hair like GiGi?" he asks as he stands and shakes the bottle with all his little might.

"No, sweetie. I don't think I can pull off blue hair like GiGi can." Plus, it would draw attention I don't need.

He smiles up at me and holds the bottle out to me. "I think you'd look cool."

"Thank you. Maybe one day, but not today."

I set the applicator tip to the part in my hair and draw a line of hair color from the back of my head to the front. The dark contrasting greatly against the pale blonde.

Closing my eyes, I take a deep breath and let it out slowly. Without thinking about it, I finish coating my hair until it's covered with the dark brown color and smelling up the bathroom.

Beckham looks up from Chewy and wrinkles his nose. "It stinks, Mama."

"I know it does, but it's part of the process. In twenty minutes, I can rinse it out and we can leave. How does that sound?"

He nods, going back to playing with his polar bear as he leans against the wall by the sink. I want to set the timer on my phone, but quickly realize I don't have a phone. Luckily,

I have a watch my parents gave me from one of their trips abroad to time myself with.

Twenty minutes later, I'm putting my head under the faucet and having Beck hit the top of it since the water keeps turning off every ten seconds it seems. Without a hairdryer, I pull my hair up into a ponytail, unwilling to squat in front of the hand drier until it's dry.

I clean up as best as I can, making sure not to leave any stains from the hair color. Throwing the color and the hair I cut off in a plastic bag, I shove it into the bag, not wanting to leave evidence of my transformation behind.

When the bathroom looks more spotless than it's probably been since the place opened, I squat down in front of Beckham with the best smile I can muster on my face.

"Are you ready for an adventure?"

His blue eyes light up. "Are GiGi and PopPop going to be there?"

"Not right now, baby." I pull his hat down a little further on his head. "We're going someplace where no one knows us."

"I won't have any friends," he pouts, but quickly looks down at his stuffed polar bear. "Except you and Chewy."

"You'll make new friends in no time. The only thing I ask is you don't tell them about Bradley."

His nose crinkles as he shakes his head.

Standing, I hold my hand out for him to take. My eyes well with tears when his little hand takes mine. No little boy should have to be put through this. What kind of life is a life on the run for a seven-year-old?

When we step outside the bathroom, a few people are milling around, but everyone is keeping to themselves. I make sure to keep my distance and my head down as we make our way out to the bus and our new life.

Stepping onto the bus, I look back at Jackson, Mississippi and wish it farewell.

"I hope to never see you again."

ONE
DELILAH

"SHIT," I curse as my driver pulls up outside the school and there are no cars in sight. I'm late on Beckham's first day of school. Could I be a worse mother? First, I make him leave the only home he remembers, drag him away from his friends, and won't let him talk to them in fear that he might accidentally mention where we've settled down. Now he probably thinks I've abandoned him.

"Would you like me to wait?" the driver asks as I hand him a twenty.

I look at the school again and see no one. Who knows how long it will take me to find my son? "No, thanks," I answer as I pop out of the taxi. Lucky for me, the school isn't too far from the women's shelter we're staying at.

Striding up to the door, I try to open it only to find it locked. I curse myself again for being late. I couldn't believe I let time get away from me, but I really thought I might land a job today. I want to get Beckham and me out of the shelter and into our own home as soon as I possibly can, but at this rate, it doesn't seem like it's ever going to happen. Perhaps it's the fact the makeup I borrowed from one of the women at the shelter doesn't do a very good job of covering the bruising around my eye that has now turned a lovely bluish-purple.

They all probably think I'm drama with a capital D. I don't blame them. I have little to no job experience, and can only work the hours Beckham is in school until I have some money saved up and can afford either a babysitter or an after-school program. The weight of it all has made me want to break down in tears more than once.

Circling the school to find another door to enter with, I find Beck outside with his face pressed up against the fence as he watches a group of older boys play baseball.

I'm not sure where he gets his love of baseball because it certainly isn't from me. I can't even remember a time when Bradley ever had the TV on a sports event.

Coming to stand beside him, I wrap an arm around his shoulders and watch the boys with him. "Hey, buddy. I'm sorry I'm late. I promise it won't happen again."

He shrugs and continues to watch them play. "It's okay. I like watching them play."

The feminine sound of a throat clearing has me turning around to see a pretty blonde standing with her purse on her shoulder and a kind smile on her face. She steps forward with her hand out. "Hi, you must be Mrs. Williams. I'm Beckham's teacher, December Black."

"Hi," I greet her, shaking her hand. "I'm Delilah Williams. It's so nice to meet you. I'm so sorry I was late. I swear I'm not normally a late person, but I'm out trying to find a job and time got away from me."

"That's okay. It was only a few minutes, and Beckham reassured me you'd be here soon."

"At least I got a new phone. My other one… broke, and I had to get a new plan and everything, but now the school will be able to get ahold of me if anything happens."

Her smile is still sweet but strained at the corners as if she can detect my lie. "Yes, they do like to have a phone number on record. Beckham was no trouble, though. He stood and watched the boys play baseball. Even though he's only been in my class for one day, he really is a sweet kid."

"Thank you. I think so too."

Squatting down to eye level with him, December asks, "Were you on a baseball team back where you used to live?"

He nods enthusiastically. "It's my favorite."

"You know, my son is coaching an after-school baseball team. Would you be interested in it? It's only one day a week, but it's free. It starts tomorrow if you'd like to sign up."

"Tomorrow you say?" I frown, unsure if it's a good idea. "I'll think about it. Is there something I need to sign?"

"Yes, but you can always do it after he signs up if that helps."

Picking up Beckham's backpack off the ground, I sling it over my shoulder. "Thank you. We need to get going, so say goodbye to Mrs. Black."

Beckham looks from me to the baseball field with sad eyes. I hate to make him leave, but we need to get back to the shelter so I can help with dinner. Tonight is my night and I can't be late for two things in one day.

"I know you two are new to town and I'd like to invite you over for dinner tomorrow night. My son will be there, and he can tell you more about the baseball program."

Taking a step back, I take Beck's hand in mine. While his teacher seems nice, I feel like she's taking pity on us. How often does she invite her student's over for dinner?

"That's a very kind offer, but I would hate to impose." The weight of Beck's hand in mine makes me look down at him. His blue eyes are brimming with tears. I can't say no if it's going to cause him such sadness. The change in our lives has already been too hard on him. He went from living in a house most would consider a mansion to now sharing one room with me where we have to share a tiny bed. If something as small as having dinner with his teacher will make him happy, I'll do it.

"We'd love to come to dinner," I finally agree.

"Perfect." December smiles brightly. "I'll put a note in

Beckham's backpack tomorrow with our address and the time."

I smile weakly at her. I know proper etiquette would be to bring something for dinner, but I only have a small amount of money for us to get by on until I get a job. What little money I do have, I want to use it for rent on a place for us and I'll need every last dollar I have for the baby. I didn't have time to get any money out of the bank before we left. Never once did I think I'd be afraid for my life when I met Bradley, but after I saw the monstrous look on his face before he attacked me, I knew we were no longer safe. He knows I now know the secret he's kept from me all this time.

Hopefully December and her family will understand I don't have the resources after moving to a new town to bring a bottle of wine or a dish because there is no way in hell I'm telling them why we're really in Murfreesboro.

TWO
DELILAH

BECKHAM SMILES happily as we walk up the driveway of Mrs. Black's house. He's been bouncing with excitement the whole way over here, to have dinner with his teacher and meet the man who runs the after-school baseball program at his new school.

"Are you excited?" I ask as I ring the doorbell. It feels all kinds of wrong to be on his teacher's doorstep, but the sad look in his eyes yesterday broke my heart and there's no way I'm going back on my word.

The door swings open and December stands there in a pair of tight jeans and a t-shirt. It makes me happy I decided not to dress up for the occasion.

"Hello." She draws out the word with a bright smile on her face. "I'm so glad you two could come to dinner."

"Thank you for having us. It smells wonderful." Even

from the doorway, the aroma of tomatoes and garlic fills the air.

She steps back holding the door open for us. "Please come in. I hope you like lasagna."

"We love it," I answer truthfully as we step inside the house. Bradley had me on a strict diet and Italian was out. He said if I ate all the carbs I wanted to, I'd be a fat ass. My fat ass sure didn't seem to bother him when we first started dating, but the second we moved into his house, he quickly had a set of rules I needed to follow. That should have been my first indication Bradley wasn't the man he seemed, but I was in denial and realized too late what an asshole and a bad person he really is.

"I'm just finishing up in the kitchen, but dinner should be ready in a few minutes. Please relax and have a seat," December chirps as she moves through the house.

I try to follow her but have to stop when Beckham comes to an abrupt halt in the middle of the living room. "Beck, what's the matter with you?" I whisper a moment before my eyes land on an extremely attractive man sitting on the couch. His blondish-brown hair is cut close on the sides and a little longer on the top, but it's his piercing blue eyes that have me captivated.

He stands and comes to stand in front of us. "You must be Beckham and Delilah. It's nice to meet you. I'm Max." Leaning down, he holds his hand out for Beck to shake.

Beck lifts his hand in a daze and pulls it to his chest when he gets it back. "You're Max Black," he says in awe.

"I am." Max almost blinds us with his brilliant smile. "Are you a fan?"

Am I missing something here? How does my son know who this man is?

"I'm Beckham, your biggest fan in the whole wide world." Beckham looks at him with an emotion I've never seen on his face.

Is this the Max Black who plays for the Yankees? Even though I know next to nothing about baseball, I do know my son's favorite player and team. Could the man before me be the same Max Black?

"Well, then, it's a good thing we finally got to meet. I'm always happy to meet my fans."

The front door opens causing me to turn around and a man who has to be Max's father walks into the house. They look almost exactly alike with the same muscular build, hair, and eye color with the exception of a few wrinkles at the corner of his eyes. Max is going to one damn fine man as he ages if his father is anything to go by.

Why am I thinking of how fine he's going to be? I just got out of an extremely horrible relationship and to top it all off, I'm pregnant with that asshole's child. The last thing I need to think about is getting involved with a man, not that he'd be interested once he finds out I'm pregnant. Not that I'm interested in any man. I don't need any more hassle in my life.

Max stands and pats the man on the back. "Dad, I'd like for you to meet my biggest fan, Beckham."

"It's good to meet you, Beckham." He holds his hand out to first my son and then me. "I'm Mrs. Black's husband, Gareth."

"It's nice to meet you. I'm Delilah. It was very sweet of your wife to invite us over for dinner."

"December loves having people over since she loves cooking. She's from a big family, and she hasn't quite figured out how to cook for only a few people," Gareth laughs.

"You can always send me the leftovers. I hate cooking for one," Max declares.

How is he single?

"You're always welcome to come over for dinner, Son."

"Are you an only child?" I ask.

"No," Max shakes his head. "I have an older brother Mitchell who's married with kids. Mitchell and Bailey are busy tonight otherwise they'd be here, and then there's my little sister Molly who's away at college."

Hearing Max speak about his brother and sister makes me miss my little sister, Ava. It has been so long since I last saw her.

"Dinner," December calls as she steps out of the kitchen with a large dish that smells heavenly. "Gareth, would you please grab the garlic bread?"

"Of course. What would everyone like to drink? We have water, milk, orange juice, and maybe some sort of soda." Gareth starts in the direction December just came from as he talks.

December and Max call out their drink orders, leaving Gareth looking at us for our order.

"I'll have a water and Beckham will have milk." I don't need him bouncing off the walls when we get back to the shelter.

"I'll help." Max follows his dad into the kitchen while Beckham sits down at the table.

"Do you need any help?" I ask, following along. I hate sitting around and doing nothing when I know I can help. I hate feeling useless.

"You don't need to do that, you're our guest," Gareth says as he places the garlic bread on a plate.

"I'm happy to help, really. Just direct me where you need me." I come to stand at the counter while Max sets out glasses for all of us.

"Is this okay for the little guy?" He looks sheepish. "I didn't know if he needed a plastic cup or anything like that."

It's sweet he thought of Beck and what he might need.

"He's good with what you have, but thank you." I take the gallon of milk he sets on the kitchen counter and pour Beck a glass and then fill one of the glasses with water from the refrigerator. "Did you want water as well?" I ask even though I heard what he wanted. I look over my shoulder to find Max checking out my ass.

He clears his throat and shakes his head a little. "Yes, thank you."

Max

I can't keep my eyes off the woman sitting across from me. She's breathtaking with eyes the color of the ocean and pale skin that sets them off even more. Her lush pink lips have me desperate to crush my mouth to hers.

I've noticed all through dinner, while she's chatted easily enough, there's strain there and I'm dying to find out why. There's also the cut on her lip and, if I'm not mistaken, the end of a healing black eye.

Looking to my left, I smile down at her son, Beckham, who's got to be one of the sweetest kids I've ever met. He looks up at me with starstruck eyes filled with wonder.

"Hey, buddy. If it's okay with your mom, do you want to go out back and play some catch? Maybe even hit the ball around some?"

It's as if I offered him a million dollars with the way he's blinking at me in disbelief.

"Can I, Mom?" he asks eagerly. His eyes and smile are so wide I don't know how she ever tells her boy no.

"That sounds like a wonderful idea while I help clean up the lovely dinner Mrs. Black made for us." Delilah's eyes land on me and she mouths thank you.

I nod to her as I stand. Beckham is already up and out of his seat. He certainly has a lot of energy for a seven-year-old. Not that I'm around many to know the difference.

Holding open the door for my new friend, I let him pass before I head around to the back of the garage to grab the baseball gear my dad always keeps on hand for when I'm here.

The moment I step outside the garage with a couple of gloves, a ball, and a bat, I see the love this kid has for baseball. It brings me back to when I was his age and my love for the sport. Never in my wildest dreams did I think I'd make a career out of it. That's why I started the program at the elementary school and chose to coach one of the little league teams. I want to give everyone a chance at their dream like I had.

We start slowly tossing the ball back and forth to get warmed up and I gradually move back, creating distance between us and increasing my speed to see what the kid has. He's good. Damn good going by the pitches I'm hurling at him. I'm not giving him my fastball, but I've had kids ten years older than him not be able to handle the pitches I'm giving him.

"Do you want to hit the ball some?" I call as I start back to him. He nods enthusiastically and runs over to grab the bat we left by the side of the garage.

"Are you planning on joining the school program or thinking about joining a little league team?" I ask as I come up beside him to check his stance. For being so young, he's got it almost perfect. My gut's telling me he's going to go pro one day.

"Do you mind if I show you a better way to stand? It will give you more force when hitting the ball." I ask because I don't want him freaking out when I touch him. I'm not sure what's appropriate or how he'll react. I'm also not sure if whoever put the bruise and split lip on Delilah, hit him as well.

He moves closer, signaling for me to show him. I only give him a few minor tweaks before he's standing in front of me perfectly. Did his dad coach him?

I don't think Delilah's married. Earlier at dinner, I didn't notice a ring on her finger. Was he who gave her the black eye and split lip? Fury courses through me thinking about a man hitting her.

"Did your dad teach you how to play baseball?" I ask as I start to move back so I can pitch him the ball.

Beckham breaks his stance looking down at his feet for only a second and when he looks back up at me, his eyes are sad and older than any seven-year-old's should ever look.

"My dad died when I was a baby. Last year my mom

signed me up to play Little League back… that's where I learned." He swings the bat, and I can tell he's impatient for me to throw the ball.

If his dad's dead, who the hell beat up his mom?

I know I can't ask any more questions tonight though. Even though he's a sweet kid, I see that he'll start to shut down if I ask too many questions. Instead, I have fun with him. It feels good to not worry about my shoulder and just play for the love of the game.

Twenty minutes later, Delilah steps outside with my dad and mom. They'd been watching us from inside, and I knew my time with him was coming to a close.

Delilah steps out into the yard and starts toward her son. "Beck, sweetheart, we need to go." His shoulders slump, but he doesn't protest. He simply gathers the glove he used earlier and places it on the table before he walks up to me with his mom coming in behind him.

He holds out his hand for me to shake. "Thank you, Mr. Black. That was a dream come true."

Damn, this kid is awesome. "You're very welcome. You don't need to call me Mr. Black, though. You can just call me Max."

He looks to his mom to see if it's okay with her, and she nods.

"I think you made his whole year if not more, so thank you. I know it really means a lot to Beck."

"Can I talk to you over here for a second before you leave?" She nods and her eyes dart to her son. I place my hand on her lower back, and she freezes, her entire body tensing for a moment before she moves off to the side and out of my reach.

I don't know if I should address the issue of me touching her or not, but when she stands there as if nothing happened, I shake it off.

"I'm not sure how much you know about baseball, but your son has real talent. I know my mom talked to you about him maybe joining the after-school program or the Little League team. While I don't know your circumstances, I think it would be extremely beneficial for Beckham to join the Little League team I coach."

"Um… I don't know." She looks off into the distance. "We're new and all, and I don't really know my way around town."

"That's okay. It's easy to find your way around. We meet up at the school to practice one day a week, although I'm thinking of making it two, and then there's usually two games on the weekends. It's at the park near the school, so it shouldn't be too hard to find."

She twists her lips and then looks back to her son. "The thing is, I'm looking for a job and I don't know what my hours will be like. Will he get in trouble if he can't come to a game?"

"No, of course not, but I'm sure someone would be

happy to take him if you can't bring him. I'll do it if there's ever a time you can't bring him."

I remember the days when it was only dad, Mitchell, and I, and I don't know how we would have got to our after-school sports or anything else we did if it weren't for my grandma and aunts picking us up and taking us where we needed to be while dad worked.

"Beck would love it, and I'd like him to be able to make some friends here. He's missing his friends from back home terribly."

The wind blows through the backyard, causing some of her hair to fly in her face. Involuntarily, my hand raises and brushes the hair away. My fingers skim along the apple of her cheek, sending electricity through my arm.

Delilah jumps back and I'm not sure if it's from the zing of electricity or she doesn't like to be touched. I don't comment on it though. Not tonight.

"We'd love to have him on the team, and I know him and the boys will get along great. Practice starts tomorrow night at six, but lots get there early to start warming up so we can get started, so everyone can go eat dinner and do homework."

"And it's at the school, right?" she questions as she brings up the Uber app on her phone.

Does she not have a car? Is that why she's worried about where the practice and games are? I'll have to figure out a way for me or someone else to offer rides for them in the future.

"You know, I'm getting ready to leave and I can give you and Beckham a ride home if you'd like."

Delilah looks up at me with her finger hovering to order her ride. "Oh, um… you don't really need to do that. I'd hate to be an inconvenience."

"It's not a problem at all." And even if it is, I'm not going to let her take an Uber home.

"That would be nice, and I'm sure Beckham will love to get to hang out with his hero for a little longer. He really is your number one fan."

"And how about you? Do you have a favorite player?"

She smiles and shakes her head as she starts to where everyone is standing by the back door. "I don't know enough about the game to have a favorite player. I'm not sure where he gets his love for it, except maybe from my dad. He loves to take Beckham to games when he can."

Interesting.

Maybe I can work on Delilah to get her to say I'm her favorite player.

"Again, thank you for asking us over for dinner. Hopefully, sometime in the future, I'll be able to return the gesture," Delilah says to Mom and Dad.

Mom reaches out and pats her on the arm. I notice Delilah doesn't seem to mind her touch. Maybe it's just men.

"Oh, it was lovely having you and Beckham over. We'll have to do it again."

My dad wraps an arm around Mom and pulls her to his side. "Yes, it was nice getting to know you and your son. I'm sure I'll be seeing you at some of the games."

His comment makes me smile. Even with me only being a Little League coach, my dad's still going to support me and act like I'm coaching a major league team.

Delilah smiles politely as she takes her son's hand.

"I'm going to go as well and give them a ride home. I'm not sure if I'll see you before the game on Saturday, but if not, it's at one o'clock." I pat my dad on the back and kiss Mom's cheek.

"We'll be there and let us know if there's anything you need. Snacks or drinks. Anything." Mom looks down at Beckham. "And I'll see you in class tomorrow. Have a good night."

"You too, Mrs. Black." His mom runs her hand affectionately down his back.

She looks at me. "We're ready whenever you are."

I want to place my hand on her lower back again and guide her to my truck, but I keep my hands to myself. I need to give her time to get used to my presence. Both my dad and I are big guys, and it's possible we intimidate her. Once she gets to know us, though, she'll realize she's got nothing to fear.

THREE
DELILAH

I SHIVER and wrap my arms around myself as the boys run around the field and pick up the equipment from practice. Even though it's late March, the sun's gone down and there's a slight wind making it quite chilly. When I was pregnant with Beckham, I was hot all the time. I certainly hope I won't be cold throughout this pregnancy. I'm sure I'll be ruing the day I ever thought that when summer rolls around and I'm as big as a whale.

The woman sitting in front of me turns around and smiles warmly at me. I'm not sure if it's small-town life or if everyone in Tennessee is this nice, but it's a nice change of pace from Jackson. "We're all going to a pizza place in town after this, and I wanted to make sure to ask you if you wanted to join us."

I want to say no, but of course, that's the exact moment

Beckham walks up to me. "Can we go, Mama? A couple of my friends asked me if we're going."

"If you want to go, we'll go." The only problem is, I have no idea where this pizza place is. I look at the mom who asked. "I'm sorry we're new and I don't know the area all that well. Can you give me directions and the name?" I hate not knowing where anything's at. I need a job so I can get a car and a place to live as soon as possible.

Although, I'll know the town like the back of my hand soon if I have to go into every business in town to fill out job applications.

"Oh, it's only a couple of miles away from here on the main road. There's a big sign that says Luigi's and you can't miss it."

I pull out my phone to order a ride now that I know it's not within walking distance.

"Mom," a little boy with brown hair and eyes pulls on her arm, "can Beckham ride with us?" He looks up at her with puppy dog eyes, making both of us laugh.

"Sure," she laughs a little before she looks at me. "Would you two like to ride with us? We've got plenty of room in our van. I could probably haul the entire team if I had to."

"I wouldn't want your van's space to go to waste," I laugh with her. "I'm Delilah by the way."

"And I'm Trey's mom, Kari. We should probably go before they turn into little savages."

I laugh because I'm all too familiar with the hunger of a growing boy, especially after they've just exerted themselves. I follow behind and wait until almost half of the boys on the team load into her van before I get into the front seat. Looking out the window, I wonder if the coach is going to join us.

Sitting back in the seat, I take in my surroundings. While it was happening, I didn't realize how much Bradley was controlling my life, but I can't remember the last time I went out with friends. He made it so I was secluded except when it had anything to do with Beckham's school or his work functions.

Kari laughs along with the boys as they rehash what happened during practice. You'd think with a season of watching Beckham play the game, I'd understand it better than I do, but there's something about baseball I don't get. Maybe I never will. I'd like to, so I can talk to him about it more, or at least know what he's talking about when he's talking excitedly about what happened.

It only takes us about two minutes to get to the pizza place. The kids race each other to the door and then wait for us, holding the door open. As we walk inside, I notice the few moms who've brought their kids to eat watch Max get out of his truck and make his way to the building. I swear I hear a few sighs before they turn to stand in line.

Arching my brow, I look to Kari, wondering what the deal is.

Leaning in, she cups her hand and whispers in my ear.

"The reason everyone goes to dinner after practice is… we all think the coach is a hottie. The few that are divorced constantly hit on him, but he turns them down gently. Still, they don't stop trying to get into his bed for at least one night."

I pull back and look to see if she's serious. Haven't they thought about how uncomfortable it would be if they did hook up with him for a night and then have to face him at every practice and game?

"It's always their idea of where to go in the attempt to spend a little more time with him and to ogle him. Don't get me wrong, there are times when you just can't help but check him out. Like now," Kari's eyes get big, causing me to turn around to see what the big deal is.

I shouldn't have turned around. Max is bent over holding something I can't identify out to a little boy. His ass is encased in a pair of very tight and worn in pair of jeans. I'm not going to lie. It's a nice ass. Now I understand what has the women making fools of themselves every week.

But the thing that I find the most attractive about him is the easy smile he has on his face while he looks down at the little boy giving him his full attention. The man may have been a former professional baseball player, but his true calling is with children.

"We're up," Kari signals as she steps up and pays for all the kids we brought, including me.

Opening my wallet, I start to fish out some money I

should be keeping when she stops me. "Don't worry about it. The parents who aren't here, pay for the ones who do attend. They already gave me money before practice, and it is far more than they needed to give me."

"Are you sure?" I question her because her reasoning seems a little fishy. No one even knew we would be on the team until we showed up. Except for Max and his family. While I don't have the money to blow on an expensive pizza place, I don't like feeling like a charity case either.

"One hundred and ten percent. Some parents on the team think they're too good to watch their kids practice or socialize with the likes of us. The parents are snobs, but their boys are sweet. I'm surprised they let their kids even associate with ours with the way they look at us. Luckily, the kids are sweet and don't think they're better than the rest of us." Kari tilts her head to the side and looks to a couple of boys who didn't ride with us and are joking around with the other boys. "Now let's go find ourselves a seat before we're stuck at one of the kids' tables."

I notice the other moms are hovering around Max as he talks to people who stop him on the way to the section we're sitting at. They really are desperate.

We sit and I try to keep my eyes off Max and the bevy of women who stand around waiting for his attention. I need to remember what happened to the last man I thought was good and the predicament I'm in now because of him. I'm single, pregnant, and have a seven-year-old.

I've got no car or house to my name, and I'm running for my life.

Even though Max seems like a nice guy I shouldn't even be looking. He doesn't need or deserve to take on my baggage. All I need to say is I'm pregnant and I'm sure he'll retreat and start looking at me like he does the rest of the moms.

Max stops beside our table and grins down at us. "Kari," he nods to her and then looks toward me. "Do you ladies mind if I sit at your table?"

"No, please, we'd love to have you," Kari responds and starts to move her purse from the seat beside her when Max pulls the chair out beside me and sits down.

"Thanks for having me, he smiles at Kari and then turns the full weight of his gaze on me. "I thought I'd see how you're settling in."

I hate lying, but I see no other way. I can't tell anyone we're staying at the women's shelter.

"Good. We haven't been here long, but I love the area and vibe of the town."

Kari raises a skeptical eyebrow. "You mean a town where everyone knows everyone's business?"

"So far, I don't mind. I come from living in big cities where you feel inconsequential. I like the thought of getting to know people and seeing them every day." While I do like the concept, I'm wondering if I shouldn't have traveled to a big city where it would be harder for Bradley to find me.

Because I do know, eventually, he'll find me. He won't give up until he's caught me or thinks I'm dead.

"Really?" Kari leans forward, placing her elbows on top of the table as she gives me her full attention. "Where did you used to live?"

Shit. I should have known there would be questions. I try to hide the panic of lying to them. I realize I should be able to tell them a little about myself without giving too much away. "I grew up in Los Angeles."

"Wow, I haven't even been out of Tennessee." Kari leans the side of her face on her hand. "Is traffic really as bad as they make it seem?"

"It's pretty bad all the time, but you get used to it. My parents moved out of the city when I was young, but we still went into LA quite a bit."

Max leans forward, his piercing blue eyes trained on me. "Do you miss it?"

"LA? No," I shake my head. "I do miss my parents though."

Earlier in the day, I sent my sister, Ava, a text letting her know we're alive, and then promptly turned off my new phone in case Bradley has her phone bugged or any type of software on there where he can read her messages.

After I turned off my phone before she could respond, I sat and cried for a solid twenty minutes before I cleaned myself up and went out looking for a job. With red, bloodshot, and puffy eyes, I hadn't landed any of the positions I applied for.

"Hey," Kari put her hand on top of mine, "are you okay?"

"Yeah," I barely say as I blink back tears. Pregnancy hormones are no joke. My emotions are all over the place and thinking about how long it will likely be until I get to see my family doesn't help matters either.

From under the table, Max drops his hand on my knee and squeezes it while he stares down at me. "Are you sure you're okay?"

"Yeah, it's these damn pregnancy hormones. They make me cry at the drop of a hat," I say as I try to play it off.

Kari's eyes get wide as she blinks back her surprise. "You're pregnant?"

I nod. I hadn't meant to blurt it out like that, but it's for the best for everyone to know now instead of them finding it out later.

"Well, how far along are you and where's the dad?"

"Kari," Max scolds, "not everyone is an open book like you are."

Kari pays no attention to Max and looks at me. "You don't have to answer if you don't want to, but if you don't, the rumor mill will fill in the gaps once they find out you're pregnant."

Max gives me a reassuring smile, giving me the courage

to give her a half-answer. "I'm not far along. I only just found out recently I'm pregnant. It wasn't planned."

"Where's Beckham's father?" Max blurts.

"He's dead. He died not long after I gave birth to Beckham while he was serving in the military. I should have gone home after that, but I was too depressed to do anything but sit at home and take care of my baby." I'm not sure if I say the last part out loud or to myself.

"So, you have a new man?" Kari looks to my left hand obviously looking for a ring.

"Not anymore. It didn't work out, so I decided it was time for Beckham and me to move on. I didn't know where I was going, but when I saw Murfreesboro, I liked its charm and thought it might be where we should set up house."

Luckily, in that moment, a server comes by to take our order. She tells us the pizzas the boys have ordered and asks if their orders are ok. I've never been to a buffet style place where you pay when you walk in and order your pizza from the table. They give you two slices of what you order, and you can keep ordering more. It's doesn't make sense, but I kind of like it. I order a couple of slices of barbecue chicken pizza while Max orders a supreme and Kari orders taco. It doesn't take long before we've each got our slices in front of us.

"Don't look now, but it seems the other moms are jealous we get the coach to ourselves tonight," Kari whispers from across the table.

Max doesn't look up, but he does smirk at her comment.

The other moms glare our way from across the room. I'm sure they're dying to know what we're talking about over here.

"Are they always like that?" I don't really need to get on the bad side of a group of jealous women.

"Can't say. Normally coach sits with a group of guys, but I guess they aren't coming tonight." Kari looks over to Max and then back to me.

"They couldn't make it tonight." He eyes me. "If you don't want to sit by me, I understand. I can get up and move elsewhere."

"Don't go," Kari nearly shrieks. "We didn't mean anything by it. I was only stating facts."

"If you're sure." He smirks before he takes a bite of his pizza.

I have a feeling Max likes the attention. While he's nice and all, I get a playboy vibe from him as well. How could he not be after being in the MLB? After my comment earlier about being pregnant, I'm sure he'll never be interested in me. Which is a good thing.

Kari tells me stories about all the moms at the other table and I get the feeling she loves to gossip. I'm sure by the game on Saturday everyone will know I'm pregnant and a single mother to boot. I'll be the talk of the town.

"We should probably get going so the boys can get cleaned up before they go to bed," Kari announces after she's told me stories about every person in the room except Max. "I'll give you a ride back to your car."

"That's alright, I can give them a ride," Max announces, saving me from having to explain that I don't have a car.

"It's really no bother." she tries to argue, but Max waves her offer away.

Max throws some bills down for a tip and heads over to the little arcade area all the boys are playing in.

Kari sidles up next to me as we wait for the boys. "Well, aren't you lucky? First, he sits next to you while we eat, and now, he's driving you to your car."

I can only shrug as I wonder if I've already lost the only friend I thought I'd made here.

"I want to hear all the details at the game on Saturday, you lucky bitch." Kari doesn't say more once Trey comes to stand beside her, bouncing on the balls of his feet. The kid seems to have endless energy.

I spot Beckham waving to a few of the boys and I can see how tired he is from across the room. I know once he takes a shower, he'll pass out for the night.

"If you want, we can wait until everyone leaves so we don't give them something to talk about," Max says from behind me, nearly giving me a heart attack.

I jump and turn to face him with my hand to my chest. "How are you so silent with how big you are?" Max only smirks down at me. "I don't think we have anything to worry about on that front. I have a feeling Kari will be spreading far and wide what she learned tonight, and no one is going to believe you are interested in a single mom who's pregnant with no man on the horizon."

"Well, if they believe that, then they don't really know me, do they? I don't think Kari will say anything though. She likes you. " Max waves Beckham over and then puts his hand to my lower back. The jolt of electricity that zings up my spine has me wanting to move away from his touch, but I don't. My mind is still whirling from his comment and trying to make sense of it.

"Hey, buddy," He ruffles Beckham's hair, making it stick out in every direction. "I'm going to give you and your mom a ride home if that's okay with you."

Beck nods enthusiastically. I love how Max is with him. It's how I wish Bradley had been, but sadly he never warmed up to my son in the four years I was with him. Again, that should have been a sign. What was I thinking staying with a man who didn't like my child or who hadn't proposed to me in four fucking years? Not that I would have said yes. At least I hope I wouldn't have.

I let Max guide me out to his truck and watch as he stands to make sure Beckham gets inside. I hurriedly get inside, not wanting him to help me. He probably offered the ride out of pity for the poor pregnant woman without a car. What's worse is I don't want to feel the bolt of excitement that runs through my body every time he touches me. I need to keep my distance from him.

Max looks into his rearview mirror and then over to me before he states softly. "He's tired."

"He is. I don't think he's been sleeping the best these last few nights," I admit. It's probably because we're sharing a tiny bed, and if either one of us moves, we wake up the other.

"Do you want me to talk to him? See if anything's bothering him? I know sometimes kids don't always tell their parents what's going on with them, but will open up to someone outside the home."

"It's okay, but thanks. I'm sure he'll sleep like the dead tonight. He's exhausted. Putting him on the team is exactly what he needed to expel some of his energy. And thanks for giving us a ride. Kari's nice and all, but—"

"You don't want to have to explain your circumstances to her. I get it. This is part of living in a small town. While you may know everyone, they will know everything about you unless you make it a point to stay private." Max turns to look at me for only a moment before he looks back to the road.

Little does he know I'll do everything possible so no one learns the reason we moved to their little town.

Max pulls up to the same spot I had him drop us off the night before. It's in front of an apartment building about a mile away from the shelter. If there had been any place closer, I would have had him drop us off there, but sadly, most of it is businesses, and that would only lead to questions I don't want to answer.

"Do you need any help getting inside?" he asks.

"We're good, but thank you. You're too kind." I lift up a hand and wave. Beckham tries to give an enthusiastic wave too but fails due to his exhaustion. "We'll see you at the game on Saturday."

Standing in the parking lot, we wait until Max's truck is out of sight and then I hold my arms open, knowing I can't ask my son to walk the mile it will take us to get to the shelter. He's already dead on his feet and I have a feeling I'll be the same once we get to the shelter.

After twenty very long minutes, I stand at the door to the women's shelter and try the door one more time only for it not to budge. I read over the sign again, only I can't see the words as I tear up, but I have the words burned into my mind.

Doors are locked promptly at nine o'clock sharp and will be opened again in the morning at eight a.m.

FOUR
MAX

I'M PULLING into my driveway with thoughts of Delilah and Beckham running through my head when Mom calls.

"Hey, is everything okay?" She doesn't normally call this late unless something's happened.

"You could say that. I just got a call from a very upset Delilah." She continues to talk, but I don't hear her. What could Delilah be upset about?

When I finally tune back in the last word I hear is shelter.

"I'm sorry you're going to have to repeat that. Why'd she call you?" Why hadn't Delilah called me? It's then I realize she doesn't have my number, making it impossible for her.

"Did you know she and her son are staying at the women's shelter?"

"No," I draw out the word thinking of the apartment building I dropped her off at twenty minutes ago.

"Well, I guess that's where she's staying. It was difficult

to understand some of what she was saying between bouts of crying. I told her I'd come pick them up, but I thought—"

"I'm on my way," I interrupt while backing out of my driveway.

"That's what I thought. While I don't expect a full report tonight, I do expect one the first chance you get. Why would she lie about where she's staying?"

"Would you want anyone to know you were staying there?"

Delilah has been pretty cagey about answering questions and now things are starting to make a little more sense, but there are still plenty of things that don't add up, and sooner or later, I'm going to get her to open up to me. Even if it's the last thing I do.

"Are they okay besides being locked out?" I ask as I start to speed down the road that leads from my house.

My house is tucked away from the town and private. Just the way I wanted it after I moved back to my hometown. The last thing I wanted was to have neighbors stopping by whenever they felt like it to shoot the shit with me.

"I think so. They're probably just tired. Can you text me after you drop them off—"

Again, I interrupt her. "I'm bringing them back to my place. I'll text you once I know they're asleep. How does that sound?"

"That's what I thought." I hear the smile in her voice.

While it took me twenty minutes to get to my house from

where Delilah had me drop them off, it only takes me ten to pull up outside the shelter. My teeth grind together as I hop out of my truck and walk over to where Delilah is sitting on the curb with her son on her lap.

"Max, what are you doing here?" She starts to stand with Beckham in her arms and I catch her elbow to help bring her to stand the last few inches.

"My mom called me and told me you called her upset about being locked out of the shelter, which is strange since I dropped you off at an apartment building a mile back. Do you want to tell me why you lied to me?"

Her blue eyes flare, but her voice is hushed when she speaks. "Can we talk about this later? I would really appreciate it if you could take us to the nearest hotel."

There's no way in hell I'm taking her to a hotel, but she doesn't need to know that. Instead, I nod and take Beckham from her and place him in the backseat of my truck. We're silent as I pull out of the parking lot. It's taking everything in me not to yell at her and then question her about why she's staying at the battered women's shelter. Now the split lip and bruising make more sense.

When we're on the long road heading to my house, she breaks the silence. "Where are you taking us?"

"I'm not taking you to a hotel, Delilah. Tonight, you and your son are staying with me. Tomorrow we'll talk about your living situation."

"You're not the boss of me. What's stopping me from

calling an Uber and leaving the moment you fall asleep?" she whisper-yells.

Leaning over, I keep my eyes on the road, but direct my voice so only she can hear. "How about the tired little boy in the backseat of my truck? Don't you think he deserves a good night's sleep? He's not going to get that if you keep shuffling him around all night."

Her blue eyes turn glassy as she stares straight ahead without answering me, her hands clenching and unclenching in her lap.

I expect some sort of reaction from her when she sees my house but get nothing. After living in an apartment in New York for most of my adult life, I wanted a place where I could spread out and when I found this house for sale, I knew it was the house for me. It's too big for one person, but I've always hoped I'd find 'the one' like my father and we'd have kids to fill it up. Never did I think the first person spending the night would be one of the baseball moms and her son.

Delilah jumps from the truck the moment I put it into park and starts for the back door to get Beckham out, but I stop her with a hand to her shoulder. "I'll get him and take him to one of the spare bedrooms."

"You don't need to do that. I'm fully capable of carrying my own son."

"I know you are, but I also know it's a whole lot easier for me to lift and carry him than you. Let me do this." I can't believe she's fighting me on this. She looks exhausted.

I hear Delilah continually huff as she follows behind me through the kitchen, living area, and then up the stairs. I pick the first door on the right to place Beckham in. It has a Jack and Jill bathroom they can share.

Delilah shuffles past me and pulls down the comforter and sheet, so I can lay her son down. I let her do what she needs to do and move to stand by the door. Carefully she pulls off his tennis shoes and socks and then pulls the covers up to his shoulders before she sweeps his hair off his forehead and places a gentle kiss there. She walks backwards, keeping her eyes on her son until she's only a couple of feet away from me. As if she can feel my proximity, Delilah turns on her heel and stares me down.

Not wanting our time to be over, I start to head downstairs. I look over my shoulder halfway down to make sure she's following me. I wouldn't put it past her to climb into bed with her son just to be difficult. I find her staring daggers into the back of my skull, and I can't help but smirk. She's even more gorgeous when she's mad. There's something about the fire in her eyes that has my cock twitching.

The second we hit the living area, Delilah rounds on me and puts her finger to my chest. "I will not have another man tell me what I can and cannot do with my child. You don't know him or what's best for him."

"I never said I did, but even an idiot could see how tired

he was. He was about ready to pass out when I dropped you off and he was asleep on you when I picked up back up. Tell me, did he walk the mile to the shelter?"

Her eyes turn to slits. "Of course, not. What kind of mother do you take me for?"

"One that lies. I don't know why you didn't tell me you were staying at the shelter. I would have happily dropped you off there."

"And then you would have asked questions. Questions I don't want to answer. Questions I can't answer," she yells, but then covers her mouth and looks up the stairs.

"I'm not going to press you for answers tonight, but tomorrow you need to start telling me some truths. And if you think about trying to leave in the middle of the night, you better forget about it. The alarm will be set and if you so much as try to leave it will go off."

Her hands go to her curvy hips. "So, we're prisoners in your house?"

"If that's the way you want to think about it to make you feel better, then yes, you're my prisoner for the night. I'm probably the nicest jailer you'll ever meet. I only want what's best for you and your son."

"Why?" she whispers as a lone tear streaks down her cheek.

Only I can't answer her question because I haven't figured out why I brought them to my house.

FIVE
DELILAH

SHUFFLING around Max's kitchen trying to find everything is a pleasant chore. His kitchen is a dream with black and white veined cream marble countertops and dark wood cabinets and floors. All of the appliances are top of the line and look as if they've never been used along with all the pots and pans. The best part is the big picture window along one wall that has a small table with four chairs around it. I could sit and look out of it for days on end.

The backdrop to Max's house is a stream with a forest behind it. I can't imagine how beautiful it is in the fall with the leaves changing colors, or in winter with the ground covered in snow.

I'm placing the last few pancakes I've made on a plate when the man himself strides into the kitchen and comes to an abrupt halt when he sees me at his counter with a spread of food put out for him. He stands before me in a pair of gray sweatpants, a tight white t-shirt, and barefoot. Damn, is he fine. Is this what most baseball players look like? If so, I need to start paying more attention.

The food I made is my way of apologizing for last night. I took out my frustrations with Bradley on him. Max has done nothing but be kind to me, and I treated him horribly.

"What's all this?" he asks, crossing his arms over his chest with his piercing blue eyes hard like ice, trained on me. I can't help but watch as his biceps bulge with the movement.

Clearing my throat, I come around the counter to stand in front of him. I have to crane my head up to look him in the eye, but I don't mind. All my life I've had to look up to my dad who stands six-foot-three and if I had to guess, I'd say Max is six-four or five.

"This is my way of apologizing for last night. You took us in when you could have easily dropped us off at a hotel and been done with us. Life hasn't been easy as of late and I took that out on you."

His eyes soften as he looks down at me. "This is the first time anyone's ever cooked in my house."

I was right in assuming nothing had been used before.

"I hope you don't mind. I thought a nice breakfast to start the day off right, might help in my apology." I indicate the pancakes, eggs, and bacon I'd made. Why did he have all this food if he doesn't cook, though?

"You've got nothing to apologize for."

Before he can say anything else, I hold up my hand. "I beg to differ. I need to leave my baggage at the door, but…" Easier said than done. Especially with realizing all the signs I'd missed with Bradley.

"But what Delilah?" He steps closer to me but doesn't touch me. "You can open up to me. I promise I won't be like Kari and spread whatever you tell me all over town. I like my privacy as well."

"Why don't we get our food and then maybe I can try to explain?" I'm not going to tell him everything, but I'll tell him enough that he'll think it's why I'm where I am now.

Max looks around the room, and then his penetrating gaze comes back to me. "Where's Beckham?"

"He's upstairs taking a shower before I have to take him to school." I look down at the time on my phone and try to predict how early we need to leave here to get to the shelter, and then school from where we are now.

"I can take him. Take you both," he amends.

"If you're sure. I don't want to be any trouble. You've already been more than kind." Surely, he has better things to do with his time than shuttle us around.

"I don't offer if I don't mean it." He picks up a plate and starts to pile food on it. "You and Beckham are never a problem, so get that out of your head."

I make a plate for Beckham and set it down at the table and then go about making one for me before I sit at the other end of the table from Max.

"I want to say this before Beckham comes down. He knows most of this, but I hate for him to have to relive it." I take a deep breath and steel myself for what I'm about to say. It will be the first time I've admitted this to anyone, and it's to a stranger no less.

"Okay," Max nods. "I'll try not to interrupt."

"Thank you. Beckham's father died when he was only a baby. I was depressed for a long time and had no idea where my life was going. I should have moved back to LA to be closer to my family, but I stayed in Biloxi where Jacob was stationed until he was deployed." I try to clear the emotion from my throat, but it's no use. It nearly prevents me from speaking it's so thick as I continue. "When Beckham was three, I met a charming man who promised to give me the world, and I believed him. I was desperate for Beckham to have a father figure and not long after I started dating Bradley, we moved into his house."

Max's nostrils flare, but he doesn't stop me. I also hear Beckham upstairs. He must be out of his shower and will soon be down, so I need to hurry up.

"I should have seen the signs of how controlling he was, but I was in denial. I was surprised any man wanted me with a three-year-old attached to my hip. The day after we moved in, I was given a strict list of rules I was to adhere to. Little by little, I slowly started to lose myself as I was kept isolated from the world. The only time I went out was to dinners where I accompanied Bradley. I was to be seen and not heard.

"It changed some when Beckham started school last year, but not for the better. Bradley didn't like the fact that I had to spend time away from the house, but I wanted to be a part of Beckham's school. I met a few moms, but we never became what I'd call friends. You'd think with us living with Bradley since Beckham was three, they would have bonded somewhat, but that was the furthest thing from what happened. Bradley would mention often about Beckham being someone else's child and I think he was jealous." I shrug, unsure why he was an asshole to my sweet boy. "I hate myself for not leaving sooner. My son is the best thing that's ever happened to me, and he's so sweet and polite. He never did anything wrong, but Bradley hated him for whatever reason. I never should have put him in a position for him to ever feel that."

Max reaches across the table and places his hand on mine. "He's the best kid I've ever met. You've done a good job with him."

"Thank you. That means a lot." I point to the light bruising by my eye. "This happened the day I found out I was pregnant." It's not a total lie, but Bradley didn't beat me up because I was pregnant, rather because of the information I'd found out about him. I only found out once I was at the hospital and they checked me out. "I left in the middle of the night. Left behind my phone, the money in my bank account, most of my clothes. Everything to start a new life without him in it, but I'm afraid he's going to find me, and when he does…"

The veins in Max's neck stand out as his jaw tics. "I won't let anything happen to you or your son. I promise you. Can I ask you what this Bradley does?" Max sneers when he says Bradley's name.

"His family is very powerful in Mississippi, and so is he." That's all he needs to know. With what little I've given him, it will be too difficult for him to figure out who I'm talking about.

"I don't want you staying at the shelter anymore." His hand that's still on top of mine tightens. "You can stay here until you get a job and on your feet. No one will come looking for you here, and if they do, I have a state-of-the-art security system."

"Max, you're too kind, but really we can't impose on you like that."

It's then Beckham comes barreling down the stairs with a big smile on his face. He sits down in the open chair where his plate of food sits.

"Good morning," Max greets him. "Did you sleep good last night?"

Beckham nods as he takes a bite of his bacon.

"What would you say if I told you, I'm going to take you to school today?" Max beams a smile down at Beckham.

"That would be the best day ever." Beckham smiles, looking back and forth between me and Max.

"I was just telling your mom, I think the two of you should stay here until she can find a job."

My eyes narrow and I'm pretty sure a hiss of displeasure comes out.

"Really?" Beckham bounces in his seat.

"Why not? I've got plenty of room," Max sweeps his arm in the air indicating his space. "Would you like to stay here?"

"Yes, please." My son looks at me with hopeful eyes. "Do you think GiGi and PopPop can visit?"

"We don't want to be a burden, honey, and Gigi and PopPop are on a trip right now." He hangs his head, making me feel bad for how long it's been since he's seen my parents in person. "Maybe we can FaceTime them, and once they're back, we can plan a visit."

I know once my parents learn what happened, they'll hop on a plane and be here in a day. While I want to see them, I don't want to answer all the questions they'll be sure to ask. I'm too ashamed to face them. I have been for a long time.

"You need to finish your breakfast so you're not late to class. We still need to go by the shelter, so you can change your clothes and grab your backpack for school."

"Yes, Mama."

For the rest of breakfast, I try to shoot imaginary daggers at Max, but he doesn't seem to notice. He smiles and talks to

Beckham like he didn't overstep by talking to my son about living here without me agreeing.

Once breakfast is finished, I gather the plates and start to wash them. I don't want to leave a huge mess for Max to clean up later, because there's no way in hell we're staying here with him.

Looking over my shoulder, I find Beckham and Max looking out the picture window while pointing and talking. "Honey, go grab your shoes and anything else you left upstairs, so we can leave in a few minutes. You don't want to be late."

When Beckham runs out of the room and up the stairs, I turn on Max. "After we drop him off at school, we need to continue this."

"There's nothing to continue. I have the space and security to house you. If you want to help, you can keep cooking me meals like you did today. Other than when my mom cooks for me, I don't get many home-cooked meals."

"We can't."

"Why not? I don't see what the problem is. I'm nothing like your ex-boyfriend, I promise you. I can promise you won't be in my way, and I'll stay out of yours if that's what you want." He moves closer until he's only a few inches away. "It gets lonely here and I could use the company. Plus, it's only until you get back on your feet. Let me ask you something. Does Beckham have his own room at the shelter?" I can't form the words to speak, so I only shake my head. "Does he have his own bed?" Again, I shake my head. "And how big is this bed the two of you share?" I clamp my lips together, knowing what he's going to say after I answer him.

"A twin," I mumble.

"Surely you'd rather have your son have his own bed to sleep in at night. And yourself?"

Damn it, if he isn't right.

SIX
MAX

I CAN'T KEEP the smirk off my face as Delilah huffs around the small room she and Beckham have been staying in. After seeing the tiny space they've called home since they arrived in Murfreesboro, there's no way in hell I'm letting them stay here.

There's also the fact that I can feel that she's not telling me everything going on with her ex, but I can be patient and wait for her to open up to me. Whatever it is, I sense it's bad after what she told me earlier this morning.

There's this profound need for me to protect them from all the ugliness they've endured now that they're in my life.

"This really isn't necessary," Delilah hisses.

"It is since you're staying at my house. How many times do I have to say it before it sinks into that thick skull of yours?"

"If you think it's so thick, then why are you bothering?"

She stops her packing and turns to glare at me. "We'll only be a nuisance. Do you really want a pregnant woman and a seven-year-old under your roof?"

After what she said about Bradley never really liking her son, I can see why she's concerned, but she doesn't need to be with me. That kid is the best damn kid I've ever met.

"Like I said before, I wouldn't have mentioned it if I didn't mean it. You and Beckham will be no problem. Plus, think of how much easier it will be to take him to games while staying with me since you don't have a car."

"I feel like you're using my situation against me to get what you want. What that is I don't know yet, but what I do know is I don't like it."

She's right in the fact I'm using it against her, but not to make her feel bad about herself. Rather, to convince her that staying with me is the best thing for her.

"Hey," I say, stepping up to her and placing my hands on her upper arms, "I don't fault you for what you've done. Now that I know the story, I commend you for leaving the way you did. I'm being a good human being and only want to help you and your son. What's wrong with that?"

"Ugh," she huffs and turns around in a circle. "There's nothing wrong with it, but I don't like the way you've gone about it. You didn't ask me, and instead, you told me what I'm doing and I'm not going to have another man dictate my life. Not now or ever again."

I can respect that. She didn't have it easy with her ex, and

I'm causing her to think about him and the way he treated her. I need to change my approach with her if I want her to cooperate without getting angry. The only problem is I like it when she gets mad at me. The way her cheeks flush and the way her nose crinkles when I say something she doesn't like.

There's something about her that draws me to her, and all I want to do is protect her from the world that seems to have beaten her down.

"That was never my intention, and I'm sorry. I don't want to run your life, but to make it easier for you. It's that simple. Now finish packing, so we have time to stop by the grocery store on the way back to my house."

At least Beckham's at school and didn't have to witness this. She's been fighting me since the second we dropped him off.

Her hands go to the curve of her hips and it has me imagining what it would feel like to have my hands on her supple curves. "You're doing it again."

What can I say? I can't help myself.

Instead of saying something that will probably piss her off more, I keep my mouth closed and help her finish putting her things into the one bag she has.

"Is that it?" I ask once she's stripped the bed.

"I know it's not much, but yeah, as of right now that's all of our earthly possessions." She looks down at the bag and then up to me with a sadness in her eyes that wasn't there earlier. "It's sad, isn't it?"

"It's not sad. I find it very commendable you took control over your life. I know it couldn't have been easy for you, especially with a young child and being pregnant. If you want, I can ask around about who's the best doctor for you and your baby."

She places her hands on her flat stomach. "That would be really sweet of you. Once I find a job and save a little, I want to see a doctor."

I don't tell her there's no way I'm going to make her wait to receive the care of a doctor until she can afford it, since I know all it will do is start another fight. Even though I like that she's a little spitfire, I understand Delilah and her pride.

Delilah leaves with the bedding and comes back empty-handed. For a moment, she looks around the room with a small smile on her face. "I'm ready if you are."

I feel a sense of pride radiating off her and she should. Delilah took back her life when she left that asshole.

We both go to pick up her overly stuffed bag, but I push her hands away and take it. There's no way I'm going to let her carry something so heavy when I'm standing right here. She narrows her eyes at me, but there's also a slight uptick of her lips. Instead of fighting with me, she picks up a stuffed polar bear and hugs it to her chest.

"I'm surprised Beckham didn't wake up in the middle of the night looking for this guy. He normally can't sleep without him," she says as she follows me out of the room.

She waves to a few people but doesn't say goodbye to anyone.

Still, she did tell them she's leaving and didn't say she'll be back, so that's a step in the right direction. That is, until I stop her from opening the truck door.

"Let me be chivalrous, woman," I laugh down my nose at her.

"And here I thought chivalry was dead." She laughs with me as she lets me help her up into her seat.

"You know, if you want to look for a job, I have an extra car in my garage you can use. It will help you save money instead of taking Ubers everywhere."

She turns in her seat to look at me. "I was walking to most of them, and maybe that's why I didn't get the job because they saw me walking. Either that, or the bruising on my face, or the fact that I'm pregnant and will only be able to work for several months before I have to take maternity leave. Anyway, if we're staying at your house, there's no way I can walk anywhere, so I might just take you up on your offer."

I smile to myself. It's nice when she gives in easily.

"If you tell me what type of job you're looking for, maybe I can help you." I shrug.

She lets out a defeated breath. "Anything, really. I need to make some money before this baby is born. They're not cheap." Turning to look out the window, she rests her forehead against the glass as she speaks. "I had plans to go to college but got pregnant at eighteen. My boyfriend at the time joined the Marines and told me he'd happily take care of his family. I stupidly moved away with him all so I could stay home and play the part of the little housewife instead of going to college. The next thing I knew, Jacob was dead, and I was alone at the age of nineteen and a single mom."

Fuck, that couldn't have been easy. It has me thinking if she was eighteen when she got pregnant that had to make her twenty-five to my thirty-two years of age.

"Did you love him?" I hear myself ask.

"I did love him, but I was never in love with him if you know what I mean."

"No, I don't." I turn to look at her and find her staring back at me. "Can you explain it to me?"

"You know how if you're around someone long enough, you begin to love them. Even if it's a friend. After years of being friends with someone, you can love them. Well, that's kind of what happened with me and Jacob. I got pregnant the summer after I graduated high school and while my parents didn't demand anything of me, I wanted to show I was responsible, so I left with Jacob. I thought I was doing the right thing, even if it did break my heart and the hearts of my parents and sister with me moving to Biloxi."

She wipes a tear that escapes as it starts to trail down her cheek. "I never got the chance to fall in love with him. He was deployed not long after we moved. I love him for giving me Beckham because he's my everything. I had severe postpartum depression after I had him, and to learn that the father of my child was dead sent me spiraling."

"Didn't anyone know?"

"My parents had their suspicions, but I told them I was fine when I wasn't. If I could do it all over again, I would have gone back home to live with them after Jacob died, but I still wanted to prove myself. If you ever meet my parents, you'll wonder why I made the decisions I did and all I can say is I was young, dumb, depressed and wanted to show them I could be something."

She's right. Her situation doesn't make sense to me. "Why do you have something to prove?"

"My parents are, well…" She shrugs and breaks eye contact. "They're kind of famous. They're not crazy millionaires or anything like that, but they are where they are today because of hard work. My mom is a famous photographer, and my dad was a male supermodel. He doesn't model much nowadays, and he became a photographer as well. They travel all over the world for photoshoots. More so now that me and my sister don't live with them. It's a lot to live up to, even if they've never said I had to. I feel the pressure."

Reaching over, I take her hand in mine. "Thank you for opening up to me. I know it wasn't easy, but maybe you'll see once you start it gets easier in time."

"Maybe," she shrugs, and goes back to looking out the window. "I know I'll never do anything like them, but I'd be happy to even have the relationship they have. My parents are more in love today than they were when they got married."

I know exactly how she feels. My mom and dad are the same way, as is everyone in the Mayson family. They are couple goals for sure.

"That's a lot to live up to, but you shouldn't compare yourself to them. I'm sure if you asked, they'd tell you they're proud of the woman and the mom you are. I may not know you very well yet, but I can tell you are a wonderful mom and you'd lay down your life for your son."

"I would. I really would." Her voice breaks as she says the last. Pulling her hand from mine, she wipes her eyes. "I'm sorry I'm so emotional. I'm not typically this bad, but this time my pregnancy hormones have taken over."

"If you say so," I joke. I like a woman who isn't afraid to show who she is or what she's feeling. It's better than the fake women who tried to surround me when I lived in New York.

"That's enough about me." She clears her throat, and her tone is more upbeat when she asks. "Have you ever been in love?"

"Can't say that I have. It's been hard to find women who are… genuinely interested in me, I guess you can say."

She tilts her head to the side. "What do you mean?"

"Being a professional athlete, women only want me for my money or status. They don't care to get to know the real me. Especially when they learn I had a short career because of my shoulder and then that I wanted to move back to Tennessee. After a while, I stopped trying to find someone to spend my time with and only sought them out when I needed a release."

"Oh," Delilah shakes her head and then clears her voice. "I didn't know we were diving that deep into our sexual history." She laughs and then covers her mouth.

"I don't want to lie to you. That's not who I am and going by what you've told me, I can surmise you've slept with the two men who've gotten you pregnant."

"A regular Sherlock Holmes over there." She giggles. "But please don't feel the need to tell me about all the women you've slept with. I don't need those numbers."

She probably thinks I've slept with hundreds of women, but she'd be wrong. I have quite a few under my belt, but I was never one of those guys to sleep with a different woman every night.

Raising my brows at her, I chuckle. "If you ever want to know, all you have to do is ask."

"That will never happen." She looks at me when I turn off my truck at the grocery store. "I still don't understand why you have all those groceries when you don't cook."

"I never said I don't cook. I just use the microwave for all my cooking needs. It's fast and simple. I never saw the point of making much when it's only me. It's kind of sad. When I lived in New York, I had all my meals delivered to my house, so it wasn't—"

"As sad," she answers for me.

"Exactly. I got used to living the bachelor life."

"And yet you want us to stay at your house." She shakes her head. "It doesn't make sense."

"Does it need to?"

She looks out the window and bites her lower lip. "If this was before Bradley, I would say no, but I have Beckham and a baby to think about as well as myself. Right now, I'm having a hard time trusting men."

I don't blame her. She's been burned badly. Being abused and controlled for the last four years would make anyone hesitant to trust new people.

"I'm going to lay this out for you because I don't want it to blindside you later. I like you, Delilah, and I like your son. From the moment I laid eyes on you, I've felt a pull to you that I can't explain, and I want to investigate it further."

She opens her mouth to what I'm sure is going to be her politely turning me down, but I stop her with a finger to her plush lips.

"I know now isn't a good time in your life, but let me get to know you and you can do the same with me. We'll take it slow and if you see me as only a friend, I'll try to learn to accept that fate."

Her mouth opens and closes a few times before she finds her words. "I'm not saying I'm considering what you've just said, but I want to know. How can you want a relationship with a woman who has children that aren't your own?"

"You know December isn't my real mom. She's my stepmother, but she's treated me and my brother more like a mother than our biological one ever did. Blood doesn't make a parent. Love does, and I can say with one hundred percent certainty that it wouldn't take me long to love your son."

Her eyes turn glassy as she stares at me from across the cab. "That has to be the single best and sweetest thing I've ever heard in my life."

"I mean every word of it."

She nods. "I know you do, that's what's so incredible about it. I…"

"What? Please tell me what you're thinking." Here I spilled my heart out to her, and she's leaving me with bated breath.

"I like you, but I need time and I'm not sure how much. I'm still coming to terms with the fact that I'm pregnant again."

"I guess it wasn't planned," I say even though she said last night it wasn't a planned pregnancy.

"You'd guess right. There was never an instant when I wanted to have his baby, but that doesn't mean I won't love it. I already love him or her."

"I never doubted it for a second. You're a good mom, and I'll give you the time you need as long as you can tell me I'll eventually have a chance."

She doesn't say the words as if she's too afraid to say them, but she gives me a timid smile and nods. That's all I can ask for in that moment. I need to show her I'm someone she can trust and someone who will be good to her, her son, and her unborn baby.

I wish I knew the magic spell that would help me break through to her. I may have seen glimpses of her softening to me, but there are more times than not she's had her walls up around me.

SEVEN
DELILAH

"MAMA," Beckham shouts from the back door of Max's house, "there's a dog out by the creek and I think it's hurt."

He sounds so sad that the poor puppy might be hurt that I set down the dish I was washing, and head to the door where my son stands. His eyes are transfixed on what looks to be a German Shepherd. A big German Shepherd, and even from here I can see there's blood on its hindquarters and it's limping.

"Stay right there while I get a few supplies," I order him. Beckham has never met a dog in his life that he doesn't instantly fall in love with, but he's never encountered one that's hurt either. Neither have I, but I've heard stories and I know we need to be cautious.

I run back to the kitchen to grab a towel, and the bowl of leftover taco meat from dinner to make the dog want to be near us when it's hurt. When I get to the door, I don't see

Beckham there, and my heart begins to sprint in my chest as I search for him.

My feet take off the second I find Beckham skipping toward the dog like they're going to be the bestest of friends after they meet. I want to scream, but I'm afraid I'll startle the dog. Instead, I try to run as stealthy as possible to stop my son before he reaches the injured animal.

Only I'm too late. To my horror, Beckham reaches out his hand to pet the dog, and I see my life with Beckham flash before my eyes. From the moment I held him in the hospital to his Little League game last Saturday.

I scream bloody murder while my feet seem to slow. I feel like I'm stuck in cement as I watch in horror as the dog bares its teeth and lunges for Beckham.

It all happens so fast. There's crying and blood. So much blood as I take my son in my arms and run back for the house. Tears stream down my face as I watch blood pump from the wound on the top of his head with each of his cries.

As I start to make my way up the steps to the upper deck, I'm stopped by an ashen faced Max. He tries to take Beck from me, but I can't let go. If I do, then I know something bad will happen to him.

"Delilah," Max says in a low voice, "let me take him."

"No," my voice is broken with tears as I clutch Beckham closer to me. "I can't. Please, you have to do something. Please," I beg.

"Head to the garage while I get a clean towel to place on

his wound." At the word wound, I sob, nearly falling to my knees. "We'll take him to the hospital, and he'll be fine."

I look up at him, but all I see is a blur. "Do you promise?"

"I promise. Now let's go," he orders.

I take a step and nearly fall, unable to see through my tears. Max catches me and picks me up with Beck still in my arms. "I've got you."

All I can do is hold him closer as Max races around his house before he sits us down in his truck. Unwilling and unable to let Beckham go, he buckles me in with my son in my lap. He hasn't stopped crying the entire time, which makes me cry harder. The pain he has to be in nearly cripples me.

"We'll be there in less than ten minutes. Just hold on there, little buddy," Max says while I hear the engine of his truck rev.

I try to blink away the tears so I can assess his wound, but they won't stop falling. I start to chant, "Please be okay, please be okay."

In what feels like a blink of an eye and also an eternity, I feel the truck come to a screeching halt in front of the hospital. The next thing I know, my door is thrown open and Max is lifting us both out of the truck.

There's a commotion of voices, but I can't make any of them out. My head feels light as I try to breathe in Beckham's scent, but it's muddled with the smell of antiseptic.

Someone tries to take him away, but I hold him tighter,

unwilling to let him go. "No," I cry out, "I need to be with my son. He needs me."

"Ma'am, we can't help your son with you holding onto him. You need to give him to us," a kind, feminine voice says to my right.

"What if something bad happens to him?" I choke out.

"We're going to do our very best to take care of him, but right now you're hindering that. You can stay by his side, but you have to let us look at him."

"Delilah," Max's soft voice, pierces through the cacophony of voices, "let them see Beckham so they can make him better. I promise he's going to be okay."

I know what I need to do, but it isn't as easy as it seems. My son is my whole life and if anything were to happen to him, I'm not sure I'd be able to go on. Still, I open my eyes and arms and let a team of hospital staff take my son away from me. Once they whisk him away, I let my head fall onto Max's chest and cry.

"You can follow us," a man says.

As if I'm as light as a feather, Max carries me and follows along. Every few seconds his hold on me tightens. When we stop, I wipe my tears away with the backs of my hands. I try to focus on what they're doing to Beck, but I can't see past all the staff.

Max starts to move away, making me whip my head to him and glare. "What are you doing?"

"I'm only sitting us down so we'll be out to the way and

they can better attend to Beckham. I know it looked bad, but heads bleed alot. I've had plenty of gashes to the head in my time and learned early on they bleed more than most. He'll be fine. I promise you." His big hand runs down my hair and back and then up again.

"I told him to stay at the door. I went to get the taco meat and when I came back, he was gone," I cry out, closing my eyes as flashes of what happened earlier keep looping through my head.

"Ma'am we need to take a look at your wounds as well if you could—"

"You're hurt?" Max interrupts, his blue eyes tracing over every inch of me he can see.

"I… I don't know. I don't feel anything."

A soft hand rests on my arm for a moment before lifting it. It's then that I see blood coating my arm.

Pulling my arm away, I argue. "I don't want to leave my son. It can wait."

"Delilah, none of that," Max stands and places me on my feet. "You don't want Beck to have to wait for you to get taken care of once he's done, do you?"

A sweet older woman comes to stand in front of me with a sympathetic smile on her wrinkled face. "The room right next door is open, so you won't be far. If there are any problems, which there won't be, they'll come to get you."

My eyes dart to Max and that's when I see blood

covering his light gray t-shirt and arm. "You'll stay with him, right?"

He swallows and I watch as his Adam's apple bobs. "If you don't need me, I won't leave this spot."

"I want you here if I can't be." My eyes start to tear up at the thought of not being with Beck when he needs me. Even though I know my parents couldn't do anything immediately, I wish I had my phone so I could call them and let them know what's happening. I need to hear their voices. It's then that I vow to myself when we get back to Max's house, I'm going to call my parents and tell them everything that's happened since I last talked to them.

EIGHT
MAX

AFTER FOUR VERY LONG hours at the hospital, Delilah and Beckham are finally released. Although they might have to come back to receive rabies shots if we can't find the dog that bit them. Hearing that news started another round of tears for Delilah. Not that I blame her. The night has been traumatic for everyone involved.

When I heard the gut wrenching scream she let out, my stomach dropped, and my feet raced out of the house before I had a chance to even comprehend what happened. And then when I saw poor Beck and his bloody head, my heart skipped a beat.

And damn if my heart didn't ache for Delilah as she cried in my arms.

Now on the way back to my house, Delilah is leaning her head against the window looking at nothing with her puffy eyes while Beckham is asleep in the back.

I called my dad and told him the news once the nurses had reassured me both of them would be okay and had mentioned rabies. He and a few of the Mayson men are searching my property for the dog in question now. For Delilah's sake, I hope they kept their women at home. I'm not sure if she can handle the full force of my family right now.

When we're halfway home, Delilah breaks the silence. "After I get Beck in bed and I know he's asleep, I'm going to call my parents to let them know what happened."

It seems a little strange she's telling me that. It's perfectly normal to tell family when another member's been hurt.

"They're going to freak out and want to come right away." She lets out a small puff of air making the window fog up. "I don't want to cut their trip short."

I can understand that, but family is more important than a vacation.

Carefully, I take her bandaged hand in mine. She has scrapes all along her arms from tree branches, but it's the bite mark on her wrist I'm trying to avoid hurting. How had we not noticed she was bit as well? "They'll be thankful you told them. Think about when Beckham is older. Do you want him to not call you when something big happens like today?"

"Oh, god, I don't want to think of him as an adult and not living with me."

"Eventually it will happen and when it does, you'll want him to call you if or when he gets hurt."

"You're right, but I don't want to think about it right now. It's not only telling them about him getting hurt, but that we're no longer in Mississippi and why. My dad is going to want to kill Bradley."

"I don't blame him. If I had the chance, I'd do bodily harm to him without blinking an eye," I confess. I've thought about it more than once, and even thought about hiring a private detective to look into it, but thought better of it, at least for the time being.

Her hand under mine relaxes as she turns to look at me. "Please don't do that. He's not worth it."

"He may not be worth it, but you are. I know you said he controlled you for years and through that, I believe he's diminished your self-worth. You deserve to be cared for and loved, Delilah."

Taking her hand from mine, she covers her face and lets out a few sniffles, but otherwise stays quiet until we reach my house. Pulling up my driveway, I notice a few trucks so they must not have found the dog yet. Once I pull the truck into my garage, I hop out to help Delilah and Beck out. I know she'd rather carry him, but I don't want her to tear her stitches out when I can do the heavy lifting.

Only, once I get Beckham out of the back, Delilah still hasn't moved from her spot in the truck. She continues to stare straight ahead until I open the door for her. The problem is, I don't think she's waiting for me to open it for her. She's so deep in thought she hasn't realized we're here yet. If she wasn't pregnant, I'd offer her a drink to help relax her, but unfortunately, I can't.

We walk silently inside the house to the stairs. I notice some blood on the floor that I make a note to clean up before she has a chance to spot it. I stop at the top of the landing and wait for Delilah to catch up.

"After I put him in bed, I'm going to go out back and talk to my dad. He and a few of December's cousins are here trying to find the dog. Will you be okay?"

She nods slowly, as if in a daze. I know they said they gave her some type of pain medicine that's safe for the baby, but I'm not sure if it's the meds, the situation, or what.

I lay Beckham down and he doesn't move a muscle, too exhausted from the night. Turning, I expect to find Delilah hot on my heels, wanting to tuck her boy in, but she's standing at the door staring at me.

Moving to her, I carefully take her hands in mine. "I'll only be gone for a few minutes, but if you need anything you can call me."

"I don't know where my phone is," she says, almost robotically. Her gaze trained on her hands in mine.

"I'll find it and bring it up to you. Why don't you take a nice hot bath while I'm gone?" I suggest.

She finally looks at Beckham, and her eyes start to glisten in the moonlight. "Yeah," she starts shakily. "Maybe I'll do that."

"Just make sure to keep your stitches out of the water." I give a little shake to her hand.

"We've never had stitches before." Her tone is without life until she looks at me. "Will he be able to play on Saturday? It will break his heart to miss a game."

I'm not sure since it's my first-time coaching. It's not like we have a doctor on the team to give the okay like in the major leagues. "I think we'll just have to wait and see. The helmet might hurt on his—"

She nods and looks back at her son. "That makes sense. He's always loved dogs, but now… do you think he'll be scared of them?"

I want to tell her no, but who knows how he'll respond to the trauma from today. "I don't know, beauty, but we'll do our best to make sure he's not." Her eyes flick up to mine at the endearment that slipped effortlessly off my lips, but that's her only acknowledgment.

"Now, go tuck your boy in, take a nice hot bath, and when you're done, I'll be downstairs waiting for you." I want to be here for her, but I need to see if there's been any sign of the dog.

I leave Delilah tending to her sleeping boy and head out back.

It takes me longer than I thought it would to find my dad and Asher.

My dad claps me on the back and looks out to the forest. "You just missed Nico and Talon. We found the dog and they're taking it to get looked at now by July."

"Now, I'm no vet, but it looked like the dog was shot," Asher says while looking out into the woods like my dad did.

"Never thought when I bought this place it would be dangerous. I liked the privacy and the views it has." I only hope Delilah doesn't blame me for what happened. What if she wants to go back to the shelter after tonight?

"It's not like it was a wolf. A dog can get shot in town as easily as out here. How's your girl?" Asher asks, moving to look toward the house.

"I think she's in shock right now, but damn did she cry. I didn't think she'd ever let them take her boy. I only hope that dog doesn't have rabies. I can't imagine them having to go through all those shots after today."

"You've already fallen," my dad mutters.

"I think I fell for her the second I met her. What I feel for her in such a short amount of time is unexplainable."

"You don't need to explain," Asher says. "It's the boom, boy. While I don't know much about her situation, I know she hasn't had it easy as of late. She probably thinks it's happening too fast, but give her time."

"There's something she's keeping from me and I have to believe it's bad after everything else she's told me. I want to protect her, but after today, what if she thinks it would be safer to be somewhere else?" I confess what's been eating me up inside.

"Do you want me to get Cobi to look into it?" Asher asks as we start to walk back to the house.

"Do I want you to? Yes, but I'm not going to. Not right now, at least. I don't know what it is, but I've got a bad feeling about it."

"Well, let me know if you want Cobi to see what he can find out. You're certainly showing more restraint than most," Asher chuckled.

"Restraint is my middle name right now. I'm holding everything back until she's ready." We walk a couple of minutes in silence. "I want to thank you guys for keeping the women at home tonight. Delilah would have run for the hills with all of them smothering her."

Both my dad and Asher chuckle. Pulling me into a side hug, my dad pats me on the back. "They can be a bit much, but they mean well. It won't take your girl long to figure that out."

"I'm coming to the game on Saturday to meet her and the boy," Asher smirks at me. "And I'm bringing November, so you might want to warn her."

"Thanks for the heads up," I laugh. Although I think on any other given day, Delilah would have welcomed them with open arms. "And thanks for coming out to help. I don't know what I would have done without it."

"That's what family's for. Now, get inside and go tend to your woman. I think I saw her standing at the window looking out."

Fuck, I'd been gone much longer than I intended. She probably thinks the dog got me as well.

I watch as my dad and his father-in-law walk around the side of my house and into the darkness. With Delilah and Beckham here, I need to have more security lights put in place. After tonight, I'm not taking any more chances with their safety.

Sure enough, Delilah is waiting for me in the kitchen when I walk inside, cradling a cup in her hands.

"One of the worst things about being pregnant is not being able to drink. No alcohol and no caffeine. Two things that all moms need." She leans back on the counter and takes a sip of what I'm not sure.

Moving toward her, I ask. "If you can't have alcohol or caffeine, what are you drinking?"

"Hot chocolate. It reminds me of sitting out back with my parents when I was little before bed. It's comforting." She looks down at her bare feet and then back at me. "I hate that I have to call them with this news. It's going to devastate them when they learn everything I've been keeping from them."

I pull her into a hug and feel her body relax against mine.

It's something we both need after the night we had. "At first, they'll be disappointed, but if you explain yourself, they'll understand. Do you want me to stay with you when you call, or do you want your privacy?"

"Can you stay around? Don't listen but be here if I need you."

She's so damn cute. I keep it to myself though with only a twitch of my lips. "I'll be wherever you need me. Now go call your parents before it gets too late," I start to guide her to the couch. "You have to be exhausted."

"I am exhausted." She sits down and folds her legs up under her. Pulling her phone out of the pocket of the sweatshirt she has on, she stares down at her phone for a long moment before she goes to her contact list and then places the phone to her ear.

Biting her lip, Delilah looks to me as the phone rings. I know the moment someone answers because her eyes immediately well up with tears. "Hey, Mama," she chokes out. "Is Dad there with you?"

I start to move to give her the privacy she wanted when her hand darts out and captures mine.

"Hey, Dad," she says after a moment and then her chin starts to tremble. I give her hand a reassuring squeeze and then plant my ass on the couch next to her. "I have a couple of things I need to tell you both."

Pinching her eyes closed, she listens for a moment before she answers them. "I'm fine. We're both fine now. Earlier

Beck got bit by a dog and in the process, I was bitten as well. We both got stitches, but now we're… resting."

I can hear a lot of talking on the other end but can't make it out.

"Yeah, about that. I know I was vague in my text with Ava, but I had to be. I'm not going to get into specifics with you right now, but I left Bradley."

From what I can hear, her parents don't seem too broken up about it. I think I actually heard her dad whoop.

"Please don't interrupt as I tell you this next part because I'm not sure if I stop if I'll be able to continue." Her parents agree, and then she looks to me and waits until I nod in agreement before she continues. "I overheard something I wasn't supposed to and got caught. Bradley beat me up. Badly. And I had to be taken to the hospital. While I was there, I found out I was pregnant. I knew if I stayed any longer, he'd kill us, so I waited until he was asleep, and I left."

My eyes bore into the side of her head. She can't even look at me after her revelation. It's either that or her parents who are yelling.

"I know I should have told you what was going on, but I didn't have time." She shakes her head and curls her fingers tighter around her phone. "I'm in Tennessee." There's a short pause before she shakes her head. "I couldn't go home. It would be the first place they'd look for me."

She listens for a few seconds and then answers.

"I was afraid he'd somehow have your phone bugged. He very well might. I wouldn't be surprised if mine was, that's why I left it behind."

Another pause as she listens.

"I cut and dyed my hair in a bus station bathroom. I don't even look like myself," she chuckles humorlessly.

That's news to me. I scan her hair, trying to figure what color it is naturally if it isn't this dark brown. I don't know how she did such a good job while at a bus station.

"We were at a shelter," she answers, and then starts to nibble on her bottom lip. "Since we got here, we've met some really good people."

"Where are you now?" I hear a man demand.

"Someplace safe. Beck's teacher introduced me to her son, and he rescued us one night when we got locked out of the shelter. We've been staying with him."

"Oh, honey," I hear her mom say and a bark from her dad.

"No, I'm not coming home. Bradley will find me there, and I'm not going to put either of you in danger. I promise I'm safe here or as safe as I can be with Bradley and his family breathing."

That sounds ominous as fuck. What does she mean by that? Who is this Bradley? If Delilah won't give me answers, I'm going to need to find answers on my own.

"You don't need to cut your trip short. I know how much Rio means to you," she says quietly.

"You and your sister mean more to us than anything, sweetheart. You have to know we'd drop anything and everything for you," I hear her dad say.

It's good to hear how much they love her.

"Tell us where you are, and we'll come to you. I want to see you with my own two eyes that you and Beck are safe," I hear her dad say.

"Is Ava safe at school?" her mom asks.

"I think so. I did warn her to stay away from Bradley when I sent her a message. You don't have to come right away. You can finish your trip."

"How do you think we're going to be able to do anything but worry until we see you? You send us the address to where you're staying, and we'll be there either tomorrow or the next day."

"Delilah, what has that man done to you?" her mom asks, her voice sad.

"Too much, but not any longer. I'm free. I'll tell you more when you get here."

"There's no doubt in my mind," her mom answers back. I want to chuckle. There's no way she's getting out of telling her parents everything. I only hope I get to hear it as well.

"I love you, baby girl. Don't ever doubt that."

"I love you too, and I don't doubt it. Never, not even for a second," Delilah says softly as tears start to track down her cheeks.

"We're just happy you're okay, but if you need to hire

security you let us know and we'll find the best damn person on the planet to keep you and my grandchildren safe. I can't believe I'm going to be a GiGi again."

"I can't either," she says while picking at the fuzz on a blanket.

"Tell Beck, we love him, and we'll see him soon, okay?" her mom says. It's hard to hear, but it sounds like she's crying.

"I will. I love you, Mama. Thank you for not being mad." It's then Delilah finally looks at me. The weight of the world seems to have been lifted off her shoulders.

"I could never be mad at you. Once we get off the phone, I want to know the address we're going to and then I'll text you once I've got our plane tickets booked."

"I will. I promise. I love you both."

"We love you too," her parents say in unison before she hangs up.

Setting her phone down, Delilah looks to me with questions swimming in her eyes.

I know what she wants to ask. Am I mad at her for not telling me the whole truth? "It seems I still have more to learn about you."

"Yeah," she answers on a breathy exhale.

"And your parents are coming to visit."

"It seems so. If you want Beckham and me to go stay at a hotel while they're here or—"

"If you suggest staying someplace else ever again, I'm going to take you over my knee."

It doesn't escape my notice how her eyes dilate and her cheeks pink up from my words.

NINE
DELILAH

STANDING IN THE KITCHEN, I watch as Beck hovers in front of the window, waiting for my parents to pull up. Somehow, in less than twenty-four hours, they've managed to book tickets and get on a plane. I'm both excited and nervous to see them. I'm not sure I'll be able to handle the way they look at me once they see me and learn everything.

"They're here," Beckham shouts and runs to the door. If he didn't have a patch of hair missing, you'd never know from this far away, he'd been attacked by a dog. When he woke up this morning, he acted as if nothing had happened. The only acknowledgment was when he asked if he could play in the game tomorrow.

I trail after Beck out of the garage and stand back while my mom engulfs him in a massive hug. My dad comes straight to me and does the same. I breathe in his distinct pine scent and my whole body relaxes from the familiar smell.

"Why didn't you tell me you're staying with Max Black?" my dad whispers into my ear as he hugs me tighter.

"Does it make any difference?"

"Not a bit, but it would have made me feel better about your safety. It could have been some twig of a guy with a single lock on his door."

Pulling back, I laugh. "When have I ever liked men who were twigs?"

"Ah, so you do like him?" He gives me a warm smile as he cups my face. "Your mom and I were wondering about that on the flight here."

"There's nothing going on between us," I tell him.

"I've been here for all of two minutes, and I can tell he doesn't feel the same. He hasn't taken his eyes off you once."

"Probably because I was nervous about seeing you," I admit and hang my head.

"Baby girl, that guy was an asshole. I hate that he hurt you, and if I ever see him, I'll kill him with my bare hands, but I'm glad you're away from him." He nods toward Max. "That man already looks at Beck like he hung the moon."

Max does look at Beck with more affection than Bradley ever did. It warms my heart. My son has the opportunity to be with someone he looks up to, and that man treats him like he's his own son.

"Alright, you've had her long enough. Now let me get

my hugs in." My mom pushes him away but kisses him before he takes a step.

Engulfing me in her arms, my mom hugs me with her all. She gives the best hugs, and it makes me realize how much I've missed them these last couple of years.

From over her shoulder, I watch my dad pick Beck up and then hug and kiss him. He looks at his stitches and then hugs him some more.

Tears cloud my vision and I cling to my mom a little harder. "I'm sorry for being a shit daughter. I promise never to do it again."

"Of course, you won't because I won't let you. Now, are you going to introduce us to the handsome man standing over there?"

My mom always knows how to break the tension, and I'm grateful for the reprieve.

Pulling away, I take my mom's hand in mine and guide us over to Max, who's standing by the garage with his hands tucked into the pockets of his tight jeans that make his thighs look massive.

"Mom, Dad, this is Max Black. He's been kind enough to let Beck and I stay here while I try to find a job."

My dad's gaze turns to me and then goes back to Max.

"Max, this is my mom, Lexie, and my dad, Ryder."

Max steps forward and shakes both their hands. "It's a pleasure to meet you both."

"Thank you for taking them in. I'll never be able to

thank you enough." My dad goes in for some weird man hug, and Max accepts it with ease. With his brows pulled down, my dad looks at me. "Now what's this about you getting a job?"

"What choice do I have? A baby isn't cheap. I'm afraid if I touch my money, Bradley will be able to find me. He still might be able to just from us checking into the hospital last night."

Max steps forward. He's looking down, but he glances at me out of the corner of his eye. "I've already spoken to a friend, and it's been taken care of. There's no record of you or Beck being at the hospital."

"Really?" Excitedly, I place my hands on his chest and lean up to kiss his cheek without thinking. It's not until I stand back and see the smiles on everyone else's faces that I realize what I did.

"Why don't we go inside? I'm sure you'd like to rest after your long flight." Max suggests with a cocky smirk on his face.

"Actually, I'd love to take a walk around this beautiful property and stretch my legs now that I've seen Delilah and Beck are okay with my own two eyes," my mom says as she takes Beck's hand in hers and starts to walk toward the back of the house.

"I guess we're going for a walk," I laugh, linking my arm with my dad's and start to follow after them.

"Are you up for a walk?" my dad asks.

Leaning up, I kiss his cheek. He's always so worried about me. "I love you, Dad."

"Aww, I love you too, sweet girl, but you didn't answer my question."

"I am." I shrug and lift my hand. "It aches, but nothing more. I'm more emotionally drained from everything that's happened with Bradley and then Beck getting hurt. I just want my life to be easy and simple."

"Well, I'm not sure how simple it will be with him by your side." He nods toward Max.

"He grew up here, so everyone leaves him alone. Well, except some of the moms on the Little League team. They'd like to get in his pants, but that's to be expected."

He makes a noise but doesn't comment for a long moment. "Your mom probably has tips on how to deal with that. I know there were times for her when it was hard to see women throw themselves at me."

I've seen my fair share of women drool over my dad. I have eyes, and I know he's gorgeous, but he's also my dad. Still, it might be a good idea to ask my mom how she dealt with it.

"I see a lot of myself in him," he murmurs.

"In what way?" I watch as my mom and Max swing Beck back and forth. His laugh breaks through the quiet and brings a smile to everyone's faces.

"The way he looks at you is the same way I looked at your mom. He's falling for you."

If anything, my dad looks at my mom with more love. I'd love nothing more than for Max to look at me with a fraction of that love one day.

"Impossible," I scoff. "We barely know each other."

"I knew right away, but held my tongue, knowing it would only freak your mom out. Your hesitance, you get from her. It's not a bad thing, but you and Beck both deserve to have someone love you with everything they have."

I stop walking and look up at my dad. His blue eyes are trained on me, giving me his full attention. "Can I confess something to you?"

"Always," is his simple answer.

"I'm worried about once the newness wears off and I get huge, he'll come to his senses and realize what he's started. Who wants a woman who's got one kid and another on the way? That's not sexy."

Holding me by the arms, my dad looks back and forth from eye to eye. "That man fucked with you. I don't know what he did, and it's probably better that I never learn because I'm not sure I'd be able to hold back from doing something that would land me in jail." He kisses my forehead and starts walking again. "You probably don't want to hear this, but I'm going to tell you, anyway. There's not been a moment when I didn't find your mom sexy. It didn't matter when she was days from giving birth to you and your sister."

He's right, I don't want to hear it, but I do believe him.

Growing up there wasn't a day that went by that my dad didn't show my mom how much he loved her and she, him.

"That's different. I'm pregnant with some other asshole's baby. What if he starts treating me differently once I start showing?"

"Then you leave and come to stay with us. Don't stay with a man if he doesn't appreciate you. I hope you learned that with Bradley."

I nod because I did. "What if I'm not meant to have the same love you and mom have?"

"I don't believe that for a second and you don't either. You're just scared. I wouldn't tell you to give him a shot if I thought he'd hurt you. Let me get to know him while we're here, and if I think he doesn't think you're the best thing he's ever laid eyes on, I'll drag you home."

We both laugh, knowing he'd very well try. "I'll wait to see if he gets your seal of approval before I hand over my heart."

"Let's go catch up with them, so I can start judging if he's good enough for my daughter and grandson."

I hug his arm and start to walk faster, knowing he's slowed down his pace for me. With me being only five-foot-two, I don't have the leg span he does.

It doesn't take long for us to catch up. With the way my mom and Max are talking and laughing, you'd think they'd known each other for years instead of a matter of minutes.

My dad moves to relieve my mom from swinging duty, and my mom falls back to walk by my side.

She smiles at me, "He's nice."

"I know, but isn't this the worst timing?"

"Stop making excuses. All they do is hurt you and him. Be open to what he wants to give you." Her advice is so simple.

"Does he get your seal of approval?" I ask, already knowing the answer.

"He does, but your dad's probably going to grill him the entire time we're here."

"And how long is that?"

She shrugs. "I don't know. Are you ready to get rid of us already?"

"If it was up to me, you'd stay here forever."

"Live here," she scrunches her nose. "While it's beautiful, you know how much I love the ocean. Maybe you can move closer to us."

Maybe, but I doubt Max wants to be away from his family.

"We'll see." It's all I can give her.

"I bet Beck was over the moon when he met you," I hear my dad say.

Beck nods, looking happily up at his PopPop and Max.

"He's my biggest fan, but I've got a secret, I think I'm his biggest fan. He's an amazing kid."

"I have to agree. He's my favorite grandson." My dad smiles down at Beck.

Beck looks up at him with confusion written all over his face. "I'm your only grandson."

"I know," my dad smiles down at him.

My mom narrows her eyes at me. "I know there's more with Bradley, but don't ever let another man keep you away from us. I don't think we can take it. We've missed you so much."

"I've missed you too. I didn't realize how much until I saw you get out of the car. Beck wanted me to color my hair blue like yours." I laugh.

"Oh, I would love to see you with blue hair. This brown," she flips the ends of my hair, "you're still gorgeous, but it's not you."

I have to agree.

"I don't think blue hair is the way to go if you're trying to hide," I laugh.

"Probably not," my mom twists the end of her hair around her finger. "How long are you going to be hiding from him?"

That's the problem. There is no end date. It's not because I'm having his baby. Bradley doesn't even know about it unless he bribed someone from the hospital to give him my medical records. Which now that I know more about him, I wouldn't put it past him.

"Until he and his family are in jail."

"Oh, Delilah, what did you hear?"

"Nothing good. We'll talk about it later. I don't want Beck to overhear." She nods, understanding. "I do have a question for you though."

"Shoot. I'm an open book."

"How did you handle it when women threw themselves at dad?" If I'm going to do this with Max, I need to be prepared.

"At first, I never thought he'd be interested in me or stay interested." Sounds familiar. "Once I opened my eyes and heart to him, I never had a chance. Your dad is the best man I've ever known. He took care of making sure that when other women were around, they knew we were together, and once they saw they didn't have a chance and that he only had eyes for me, they backed off."

"Still, it couldn't have been easy," I push.

"If a man wants the attention of other women then no, it's not easy. Most don't have to see pictures of their significant other with someone else on their arms. It took some getting used to, but… let's put it this way, your dad always made sure to let me know I was his top priority."

I know she's right, and there's no reason for women to be on Max's arms. He's not a model or an actor.

"If you'd like, your dad and I can watch Beck one night while we're here to give you two some alone time. I'm sure you haven't had much of that."

She's right. Max is normally busy while Beck's at school most days, and I've been trying to find a job.

"I know you're worried about lots of things, but I want to give you some money so that stress isn't on you. Enjoy this pregnancy and time with Beck and Max before the baby comes."

"Mom, I can't do that. I want to stand on my own two feet."

"And you have been for the last seven years. Don't fight me on this. Let us help you for once in your adult life. Life doesn't have to be as difficult as you make it. We love you, honey, and I should be able to spend my money the way I see fit."

"You've worked so hard for it," I argue.

"Exactly, so I should get a say in how I spend it. I want to make your life better. Please let us do this for you."

I don't want to give in, but I know I won't win either. "Fine, but not too much. I'll pay you back someday. I don't know when, but I promise I will."

"The best way to pay me back is to give yourself and your children a happy life."

Damn, I have the best parents.

"I promise."

TEN
DELILAH

"RUN, BECK, RUN," my dad screams from the stands. He's standing with his hands cupped around his mouth as if Beckham can't hear him. The entire town can hear my dad as he cheers him on.

I don't fault him. It is the first time he's watching his grandson play baseball. When Max told him how good he thought Beck is, my dad nearly fainted.

"Games will never be the same after your parents leave," November giggles at my side.

I have to agree with her. If I could get my parents to move, I would, but my mom's love for the ocean will keep me from asking. I know if I ask more than once, she'd move to be closer to us, and I can't ask that of her no matter how much I want her here.

My mom looks around me to Max's grandmother,

November. "We'll come as often as we can. I don't want to miss more than I have to."

"Where do you live?" November asks.

"In California." She chews on her bottom lip for a few seconds, and then her eyes light up. "Maybe we can find a place to rent for the season, or… if this is where you're planning to settle down." Her eyes dart to mine. "We could buy a place here, and then we'll have a place to stay when we visit. I'm sure you'll want help when the baby comes."

I feel my cheeks heat as all eyes go from my very beautiful, blue-haired mom, who seems to have everyone's attention to my still flat stomach.

My eyes narrow only enough for my mom to notice. I don't appreciate her putting me in this position. She's pretty much asking me if I want to stay here because of Max, but how can I give her an answer when we haven't even kissed yet. There have been a couple of instances where we came close, only to be interrupted by Beck or my parents. It's nearly impossible for us to get a moment of alone time. "That's the plan. I would love for you to stay here. Maybe you could rent your place out when you're not here."

My dad turns around and looks down at us with a smile. "Are we moving?"

Lacing her fingers with his, she pulls him down to sit next to her. "Not quite, but what if we got a place here since Delilah is planning on staying?"

He scoots closer to my mom and holds her hands as he nods. "It's not a bad idea. A good investment for sure."

"Perfect." My mom claps. "We can start looking tomorrow. Then maybe we can get Ava here for the next game. I know she's been missing you."

I laugh. Growing up, I never thought I'd miss my baby sister, but I can truly say I've missed her. She's the total opposite of me. Ava is smart, tall, sandy blonde hair, and put together. She's in her last semester of college and I know when she's unleashed on the world, she's going to do great things.

"You do know there's a game next weekend. There's games every weekend."

Leaning in, she whispers, "We better find a place then because I doubt Max wants us cramping his style for long."

Even with her whispering, two moms turn around and narrow their eyes our way before they lean into each other. "It seems big city living has changed Max Black."

"Who knows what's going on in that house of his?" the other whispers back.

I narrow my eyes at them, but say nothing because, what can I say?

My mom rolls her eyes at them. "Don't listen to them. They want what they can't have. Remember what we talked about yesterday?"

I don't have a chance to answer her because the crowd goes wild. Beck was on second base, but now he's rounding third and coming in to score with Trey hot on his heels.

Everyone around me jumps up and starts yelling, and it makes me feel like I'm where I'm supposed to be. I want to be around people who will support me and Beck, even if it is little things like him scoring for his team.

I sit at the table sipping on a Sprite after becoming nauseous at the end of the game. All I wanted to do was go inside and lay down, but the team was so excited after their big win, I couldn't deny everyone coming over and having pizza.

My dad scoots in beside me at the table and wraps his arm around my shoulders. "Are you okay, baby girl?"

"I'm fine, just feeling a little nauseous." I tip my cup to him. "I'm hoping this will help settle my stomach."

He squeezes my shoulder. "Beck was great today. The whole team really, but Max is right, he definitely has talent. With Max as his coach, I have no doubt Beck is going to be one of the best players there is one day."

I rest my head on his shoulder. "I think you're biased."

"Maybe, but I can also spot talent, and he has it. Not to change the subject, but while I've got you alone. What do you really think about your mom and me getting a place here?"

Pulling away, I place my hand on top of his. "I would

love nothing more than to see you both more. I can't expect you and mom to give up your beautiful house with the beach and water, but I'll take what I can get with both of you."

My dad smirks down at me. "You don't miss the beach?"

"I do, but I find the beauty here too. I like the change of seasons."

"Max's place does have a great view. I'm sure that doesn't hurt."

I slap at his chest. "Are you going to be disappointed in me if things don't work out between us?"

Pulling my head back down to rest on his shoulder, he hugs me. "Not at all. I only want you to be happy. Tomorrow we're going to take Beck with us to look at places, so you and Max can have some alone time."

It's good to know my parents like Max so much. Maybe I should have listened to them more about the relationships I was previously in.

My dad pats my leg. "I'm going to give you some alone time with Max before the pizza gets here. I have a feeling it's going to be chaos once the food arrives."

"I think you're right. I don't know what he was thinking inviting the whole team over."

Standing, my dad leans down and kisses my forehead. "I think he did it for Beck. Save me a seat when it's time to eat."

"You got it." I smile as I watch my dad go to my mom

and wrap his arms around her from behind and then kiss the side of her neck. When I was growing up, I thought their affection was gross, but now it only makes me happy and yearn for it myself.

Sitting down in the seat my dad just vacated, Max leans over and whispers, "I love your parents."

"They love you. They're going to take Beck with them tomorrow when they go look for a place to buy here."

Max's blue eyes widen almost comically. "That was fast."

"I think they've fallen in love with Murfreesboro just like I did, but they're not moving here permanently. They want to be able to watch as many games as they can of Beck's and be here when the baby comes. They'll still be traveling for work and living in California. The reason they're taking him with them is to give us some alone time."

"Oh." He draws the word out. "Maybe I should ask you out on a date then. Make it official." He smirks down at me.

"Maybe. I might say yes." I shrug like there's a possibility I'll say no.

A strong wave of nausea hits me, and I fight off the need to be sick.

Worry creases the area around his eyes. "Are you feeling okay?"

"I'm nauseous. I'm hoping it's something I ate earlier not the start of morning sickness." I'm only kidding myself though. I know it's morning sickness.

The tip of one of Max's fingers skates along the side of

my leg under the table where no one can see it. "Will you be up for a date tomorrow?"

"Nothing, not even a little morning sickness could keep me away, but first you have to ask me." I raise one brow as I look at him.

Picking my hand up, he asks, "Delilah, will you do me the honor of going out on a date with me tomorrow?"

I can feel eyes on us, but I don't care. I'm not going to let them ruin our moment. "I'd love nothing more."

Bringing my hand up to his mouth, Max brushes his soft lips along the top while keeping his eyes locked on mine before he pulls it to his chest to bring me closer to him. "I'm going to kiss you now."

All I can do is nod, wanting nothing more. I want to feel those lips on mine. I've wanted it for days. Slowly, as if someone turned the world to slow motion, Max's hand comes up to grasp the nape of my neck as he leans in. The kiss is tentative at first. Only our lips touching as zips of electricity make my lips tingle with delight. I hum against their softness. My eyes flutter closed, wanting to cherish this moment for the rest of my life.

Angling my head, Max takes control as he deepens the kiss, sweeping his tongue along the seam of my mouth. Gladly, I open for him, meeting his tongue with mine. I make a move to crawl into his lap when Max breaks the kiss. He's got a lazy smile on his face, and his eyes are hooded with need. I try to make my move again when he chuckles. "Maybe we should wait until we don't have an audience."

I jump back, having forgotten where we are and who's around us. Covering my face with my hands, I groan. "I'm sorry. I…" I swallow down the bile that's slowly climbing up my esophagus.

Heated breath fans across the side of my face and neck. "It's alright, beauty. I like the fact you lost yourself in our moment. There's nothing I want more than to have you on top of me."

Clamping my mouth shut, I nod in agreement. My body feels like it's on fire, making it almost impossible for me to hold back from being sick. "I'm sorry. I've got to…" I stand abruptly, no longer able to hold back, and run inside the house.

I can hear the clamor of the guests as I dash through the house and up the stairs. I barely make it inside the bathroom and slam the door shut before my breakfast is greeting me and the toilet.

Retch after retch follows until I've got nothing left inside of me to throw up. My stomach muscles clench and ache leaving me feeling miserable on the bathroom floor. Closing my eyes, I rest my arms on the toilet seat, and lay my head on top of them, trying to catch my breath and make sure I won't start dry heaving again.

I can't tell how long I've been laying there when I hear

the door open and close. I don't even have the energy to tell whoever it is I want to be left alone.

A soft hand brushes my hair off my face, and my mother's coconut smell washes over me. "Oh, baby girl. Let's get you up and in bed. I'll get you a cold washcloth, and maybe that will help you feel better."

Doubtful, but I keep that to myself. In this moment, it's nice having her take care of me like she used to do when I was a child and sick. I listen to her turn on the water and then feel a wet, cool cloth on the back of my neck.

"Now, let's get you up and into bed."

I let her help me up off the floor. Not because I'm weak, but because I can't believe I kissed Max in front of what had to be forty people, and then ran inside and threw up. He's never going to want to kiss me again.

Once I'm on my side in the middle of the bed with one washcloth on the back of my neck and the other on my forehead, I feel the bed dip and my mom lie down beside me. She pushes aside the wet hair on my forehead and kisses my temple.

"Are you feeling any better?" she asks softly, as if one loud word might send me back to the bathroom.

"I am. Thanks. I can't believe I did that in front of Beck's whole team and their parents." I groan and pinch my eyes closed.

"I don't think the boys even noticed." My mom says

probably trying to make me feel better. What she's saying is the boys didn't see it, but all the parents did.

"I'm going to be the laughingstock of the town. Who throws up after a hot guy who's one of the kindest men they've ever known kisses them?"

"A pregnant one." She laughs softly.

Hearing her raspy laugh makes me smile. "Do you want to hear something horrible?" I ask quietly.

I feel her head come to rest on my pillow. "Of course, I do. I always want to hear anything you have to say."

"While I already love this baby, I wish I wasn't pregnant. Why couldn't I have met Max instead of Bradley?"

"Oh, baby girl," she sniffs and drapes her arm lightly around me. "I think you met Max when you were supposed to. If you had met him a few years ago, you might not realize how amazing of a person he is. You might not appreciate how good he is with Beck or you. Plus, things would have been different then because of his career."

True. I'm not sure I could have dealt with him being gone for long periods at a time, and there is no way Beck and I could have followed him around the country just to be with him.

"He's so good to us, and I don't understand why. He could literally have anyone he wants, so what does he want with a single mom who's pregnant with another man's baby?"

A gruff throat clearing has my eyes pop open to see my

mom's are wide with an amused grin on her face, and Max is standing just inside the door.

"Lexie, do you think I could talk to your daughter alone for a few minutes?"

She doesn't hesitate to get off the bed and start for the door. "I'll be out back if you need me. I'm sure the pizza will be here any moment and they'll probably need some help."

Max waits until she closes the bedroom door to make his way to me. He sits down on the edge of the bed and runs his knuckles along my cheek. One corner of his mouth quirks up. "I hope my kissing isn't so bad you had to run away."

My hand comes up and claps onto his wrist, holding it in place. "I think we both know it had nothing to do with your kissing skills."

"That's good to hear. What your mom said… I think she's right. We came into each other's lives at the right moment. I wouldn't have been good to have around before this year. I was constantly traveling for games and barely home. I would have been a horrible boyfriend."

Oh god, he heard all of that. Kill me now. And it looks like I was right about the traveling.

"Anything would have been better than Bradley. I'm so ashamed of myself for staying with him. It was like the moment he hit me, my head became clear, and I realized how much of myself I'd lost while being with him," I confess.

"I'm sorry you went through that, but don't punish me

for his mistakes." His thumb caresses my cheekbone. "I will never treat you with anything but great respect. I like the woman I've gotten to know and don't want you to change. I was raised by strong women who I believe can do anything they set their minds to."

"You say all the right things, Max. I know I shouldn't punish you for my past, but my past stood up and slapped me only a couple of weeks ago."

His jaw tenses. "I get that. That's why I've been patient with you. I don't want to push you into something you're not ready for, but I want you to know I don't care that you have Beck. He's the best kid ever and if I'm lucky to someday call him my own, it will be no hardship, but a privilege."

Moving, I curl into Max's lap and let the tears that started to well up while he spoke, break free.

"Hey, I didn't say that to upset you. I want you to know I don't care that you have kids."

"What if… what if we don't work out—"

I feel his body tense up underneath me. "We're going to work out. Get that in your head right now. Don't start second guessing us, when we've just begun."

"Okay, but what if I don't want any more kids after this?" I place my hand on my stomach and pray this won't be a deal breaker for him.

"Then I guess I'd be blessed with two kids instead of more, but don't count out having more kids yet. Let me show you how a real man treats a woman and her kids before you make up your mind."

I want to laugh at him. It's not having an absent father that would make me not want more kids, although it certainly doesn't help. It's the pregnancy and childbirth itself.

"Promise me, Delilah," he orders.

Removing myself from his lap, I roll onto my back and look up at his handsome face. I can see the determination in his piercing eyes as he wills me to promise him. "I promise, but I want you to promise me something as well."

"Whatever you want," he shoots back.

Taking his hand in mine, I look at it while I play with his fingers, unable to meet his eyes when I speak. "If you lose interest in me, Beck, the baby, or all three of us, please let me know before it's too late."

"It won't happen, but if it does, I promise to let you know." He lets me play with his fingers for a few moments before he speaks again. "Are you feeling better? Enough to go back outside?"

"I think so, but I need to stay away from the smell of food until I get over the queasiness."

Cocking his head to the side, he asks. "Did you feel like this with your first pregnancy?"

"I wasn't sick for a day of it, but from what I've read, they're all different. The only reason I knew I was pregnant with Beck was because I didn't have my period for two months."

"Maybe I should read a book, so I know what to expect. I'm new to all of this. When my mom, was pregnant with Molly, I was young and don't remember a whole lot about it."

He needs to shut up before I make him stay in here with me while he has a yard full of guests. How is this man so damn perfect?

There's a soft knock on the door before my mom peeks in. "The food's here and everyone's waiting on you to come out before they start eating."

"We'll be right out," I say as I sit up on the bed. Once she leaves, I get up on my knees and kiss Max's cheek, realizing I didn't brush my teeth after throwing up. "Thanks for coming in here to check up on me and easing my mind once again. I can't wait for our date tomorrow."

"I wish we didn't have the whole team here with their parents right now, but I'll have to settle for some alone time with you tomorrow." He dips down and I think he's going to kiss me again, but turns his head and kisses the corner of my mouth. Raising his head, his eyes lock onto mine. "Hopefully we can redo the end of our kiss and more. Tomorrow."

ELEVEN
MAX

RYDER, Delilah's dad, stares at me from across the room as he says something to Delilah. He's been glaring at me all morning as if he knows what I have planned for his daughter once he leaves. He wouldn't be wrong, but damn, I've never had a dad know my intentions before.

"Bye, guys, have fun and good luck," Delilah says as she waves them off and closes the front door.

She turns to me, her dark hair fanning out behind her, and places her hands on her hips. "What's with you and my dad?"

I lick my lips, wanting my hands on those lush hips of hers. I've been dying to sink my fingers into her supple flesh while inside of her.

Her pink lips form an 'O' before she starts to walk toward me. The sway of her hips hypnotizes me, making me unable to look at anything else until she's standing right in front of me. Only then do I lift my gaze to her face.

"Are you saying my dad caught you looking at me that way?" Her creamy skin pinks up at the notion.

My hands grip her by the waist and pull her between my legs. Her hands come to my shoulders. "If I had to guess, I'd say yes. It's not my fault you're too enticing not to stare at and daydream about."

"You sure do know how to flatter a woman, Mr. Black." She takes me in as she stands before me. One hand moves slowly to play with the hair at the nape of my neck.

Never has a woman's touch made me as hard as I am in this moment, and it's innocent as all hell.

"Maybe you'll let me use my mouth in other ways. Perhaps we can recreate our first kiss without you running off on me," I say before I pull her down on top of me, and she straddles my lap.

She looks away from me before she says. "You mean get sick."

I didn't want to bring up yesterday and her being sick. I hadn't meant for us to have our first kiss in front of God and everyone else, but I lost myself in her. Something I find I do all too often when I'm with her. The draw to Delilah is a visceral thing that I have no intention of ignoring. I pride myself on my instincts and my instincts tell me the woman looking down at me with her big blue eyes is the one for me. I just have to make her see it.

"I'm going to believe it's from the baby growing inside of you and not that I've been lied to all my life about my kissing skills." I chuckle. I've had no complaints in the past. In fact, I've only had exemplary remarks, but I'm not going to say that to her.

"Oh, I can attest you've got nothing to worry about. You're one hell of a kisser, but maybe you'd like to try it again just to make sure."

I hum, liking this playful side of her. She's finally relaxed around me and not fighting what she feels. Because I know for damn sure, Delilah feels exactly what I'm feeling, and it scares the hell out of her.

Cupping the back of her head with the palm of my hand, I pull her down to me until I can smell her minty breath and wait for her to close the distance. I'm only giving her this one last time to take control to make sure this is exactly what she wants, and after that, I'm going to consume her body, mind, and spirit.

Licking her lips, her pupils dilate until the black almost completely takes over her irises. It feels like an eternity as she eliminates the small amount of space between us, but when her lips touch mine, the world stops and takes a breath before it starts all over again.

I sweep my tongue inside her mouth and devour her as she crushes her body to mine. I can feel the heat of her pussy through the fabric of my jeans as she slowly rubs herself on me to the rhythm of our kiss.

There's nothing I want more than to lay her down on the couch and have my way with her, but I want our first time not to be remembered as desperate even if it is the truth.

Wrapping my arms around her, I stand. Her legs wrap around my waist as she breaks the kiss and nibbles along my jaw. I let one hand slide down her back and slip into the back of her leggings that make her ass look downright delectable. As I walk us upstairs to my bedroom, I find she doesn't have on any panties and she's slick and bare for me.

"Fucking hell, woman. I haven't even seen your pussy yet, and I'm already in love." I can't wait to have her spread out on my bed to taste her.

Her teeth latch onto my ear and bite, causing my dick to kick in my jeans. If there was any doubt in my mind about Delilah being made for me, that right there, washed it away.

I quicken my strides and the second I step into my bedroom, I kick the door closed and lock it. No one—and I mean no one is going to interrupt me from taking this woman.

Removing my hand from her leggings, I let her body slide down mine. Once her feet hit the floor, I'm down on my knees and divesting her of every stitch of clothing she has on until she's standing in front of me, letting me see every inch of her creamy, perfect skin.

"Lean back on the bed," I order, gruffly. Once she does as I say, I throw her legs over my shoulders, and run my hands up the inside of her thighs, and spread her wide for me. Her bare pussy is pink and glistening just for me, and I can't wait to get a taste of her.

I start my descent when she grabs my hair and stops me. My eyes dart from where I want to be and then up to her face. "Take off your clothes, big man. I want to be able to see and touch you."

I swear if it's possible my dick just grew from its already aching state behind my zipper. I'm happy free it from the confines of my tight jeans.

Standing, I don't take my eyes off her as I remove my t-shirt and start to unbutton my pants. Delilah gets up on her elbows and watches hungrily as I slowly slide my jeans down my thighs, taking my boxer briefs with them. My hard cock springs free and slaps against my stomach. I can feel a drop of pre-cum make its way down my shaft as I step out of my pants and toss them to the side.

From the hungry look in her eyes, I can tell she likes what she sees, but I still ask. "Do you like what you see, beauty?"

Biting her bottom lips, she nods and motions for me to come closer. As if she had to ask. I'm about two seconds away from diving into her pussy and nothing is going to stop me.

Kneeling at the end of the bed, I hook her legs over my arms, making her open wide for me. I look up to find her still up on her elbows watching me. "Let's see if you taste as good as you look."

Sweeping down, I flatten my tongue as I lick her from

back to front in one long lick. The taste of her honey has me plunging my tongue deep into her core to get an even better taste. Delilah's hips shoot off the bed and she lets out a breathy moan.

Throwing one leg over my shoulder, I suck on her lips and swirl my tongue around her tight bud before I go back to fucking her with it. I can't get enough of the way she tastes. She's the finest honey I've ever partaken in.

My thumb moves to circle her clit as I lick along her folds and back inside. She writhes against my face, wanting more and I oblige. Switching, I dip two fingers inside and start to pump and use my tongue to lick and circle around her bundle of nerves. When her legs start to shake and she grinds her pussy into my face, I slip a third finger inside, stretching her wide and suck hard on her clit.

One hand pulls at the short strands of my hair while the other grips my bicep like she never wants to let me go.

Delilah's back arches as her legs clamp around my head, silently begging me not to stop, and I don't. I keep pumping and licking as her walls clamp down on my fingers. Slowing my fingers until they're sliding in and out of her in languid strokes, I bring her down. Slowly her body starts to relax into the bed, and she lets out a little purr.

I place a kiss on her inner thigh and crawl onto the bed. My arms wrap around her as I bring us both up to the top of my bed where I leave her to catch her breath. Delilah's eyes are closed, and she has a serene smile on her face. Without opening them, she turns her head to me. "How am I ever going to get anything done now that I've felt your mouth on me? If I'm not forcing you between my legs, I'm going to be daydreaming about it."

Bringing myself up onto my elbow, I look down at her and chuckle. "You haven't seen anything yet." Dipping down, I run my tongue along the seam of her lips, needing another taste of her. She opens and sucks my tongue into her mouth.

One second I'm tasting and relishing every part of her mouth and the next she pushes me onto my back and is on top of me. I'm not going to complain though. I like the sight of Delilah sitting on me with her heavy breasts there for me to touch, suck, and weigh.

Reaching around behind herself, Delilah takes me in her hand and starts to stroke as she rubs her ass on me as well. "Tell me your clean," she pants, her blue eyes intense as they stare down at me.

"Yeah," I nod, my hands reaching up and pinching the pink tips of her nipples. Fucking hell if I don't want to slip inside of her bare. In all my years, I've never been with a woman that way and now I know why. It's meant to be with Delilah. "I want to be inside of you without anything between us," I husk out. I don't even recognize my own voice it's so coated with need for her.

Without a word, Delilah raises up and positions me at her entrance. Never once does she break eye contact as she slowly sinks down on my length. Once she's fully seated, she tilts her head back and moans the most exquisite sound I've ever heard in my life.

With her hands on my stomach, she starts to move up and down and rocks on my cock. "You're so damn big. I feel like I'm going to split in two. I need…" she says breathlessly and starts to move a little faster.

Knowing what she needs, my hands move on their own accord. One goes to her hip to help her move while the other moves between her legs. I make slow circular movements with my thumb on her clit and feel her walls flutter around me. I've never seen anything hotter than this woman who's riding me and using me for her pleasure.

Each time she comes up, my hips follow her, wanting my cock deep inside of her at all times. When she starts to swivel her hips as she meets the base of my shaft, I nearly lose my load. Holy fucking shit, she's going to unman me in a matter of minutes. But I can't hold back. Everything about her makes my body feel more alive than it ever has, even out on the field. Every nerve ending is sparking to life as pleasure and heat course through my body.

"Fucking hell, you're a dream come true. Ride me and let me coat your insides with my cum." From underneath her, I start to pump my hips faster. I coat my thumb with her juices and rim her tight hole until she starts to press back against the pressure. When her walls start to flutter, I press inside, making her heat pulse around me and milk my cock.

Sitting up, I drive into her. Taking her mouth with mine until she breaks away, and lets out a heady moan that has my cock jerking inside of her and letting stream after stream of my seed coat her insides.

Delilah goes limp against me while I pump in and out of her, drawing out the last of our releases. She'll be lucky if I ever let her out of my bed again, and if she fights me, I'll tie her down until she's my willing slave.

TWELVE
DELILAH

I'VE ALMOST FALLEN asleep when Max slaps my ass and sits up with my body draped across his. I must make a sound of protest because he chuckles and squeezes me tight.

"As much as I would love to stay in bed with you all day, I promised you a date and I'm a man of my word. Plus, your dad might kill me if they come back, and I've got you naked in my bed."

Lifting my head, I smile at him. While Max is always handsome, right now with his hair a mess, completely naked, and a relaxed smile on his face, he looks younger and even more gorgeous than normal.

Running my fingertip over his full bottom lip, I ask, "How is it you look better after sex while I'm sure I look like a complete mess?"

Leaning in, he touches his nose to mine. The feel of his hot breath skating across my face has me closing my eyes and willing my body to calm down. "If this is you messy, I don't want to see you any other way." He climbs off the bed with me in his arms as if I'm as light as a feather and carries me into his bathroom. "Get cleaned up, so I can take you on our date."

It's sweet he wants to take me out when we have the whole house to ourselves when I'm not sure the next time we'll be alone is.

He sits me down on the cool counter and leans a hip against it as he looks me over. His eyes are half-lidded when they meet mine. "Wouldn't it be easier if I got ready in my own bathroom?"

"This is your bathroom now. I don't want you staying in the other room. I want you in my bed every night."

I tilt my head to the side and take him in. He's serious, and I'm not sure how I feel about it. How will Beckham feel with me not being in the room next to his? And my parents are here.

Biting my bottom lip, I look down at the toenail polish that's starting to flake off. "Isn't that moving things a little too fast?"

"Did you not like being in my arms only a minute ago?" He crosses his arms over his chest, and I can't help but watch his muscles with the movement.

"I did."

"And did you not like fucking me?"

"I more than like it, but—"

"But what? We're grown adults and I don't want to waste time on something when I know it's going to happen down the line, anyway."

The way he talks about us is unlike anything I've ever experienced in my life.

"What about Beck? He's used to being right next door to me." I try to reason with him.

"Tell him where you'll be and if he needs you, he can come to you. If you want, we can sit down with him and see how he feels about us being together."

Leaning forward, I take his hand in mine. "You'd do that?"

He steps to me and brings his other hand to my waist. His thumb rubs circles on my hip. "When are you going to realize I'd do just about anything for you? If it will put your mind at ease, I'll happily talk to him." His face hardens for a moment before he speaks again. "Did you share a bed with the asshole who hurt you?"

I did, but I don't want to voice it. I'd like to not think about Bradley for one day.

He must take my silence as an answer. "If Beck doesn't like it, we'll figure something else out, but I want you in my bed."

I'm not sure if it's because he's older or because Max is Max, but I love his confidence in us. He doesn't try to fight me but explains himself so I can see his reasoning. Each day

I spend with him, I fall a little more for him. I only hope he doesn't let me fall flat on my face.

"I don't know about you, but I'm hungry."

Excitedly, I jump down. I can't remember the last time I went on a date. Looking over my shoulder as I turn on the shower, I ask. "What are you going to do?"

"I'm getting as far away from you as possible, so I don't take that fine ass of yours from behind and we never make it out of the house. Meet me downstairs when you're ready."

I watch as he walks into his closet before I step inside. The hot water coming from the pulsating beat from Max's showerhead feels like a dream. I could stand under the spray all day, but when I see Max walk out of his closet and his eyes land on me, I rush to clean up, being mindful of the stitches on my hand. I'm not sure what he has planned, but whatever it is, I hope it leaves some time for sex before my parents get back.

I'm not sure what they're going to think about me moving into Max's room, but I have a feeling they'll understand. Their top priority is my happiness, and Max makes me happier than any man ever has.

As I step out of the shower, I see Max come out of his closet again, and wonder what he's been doing since he's in the same clothes he walked out in earlier. After quickly drying off, I wrap a plush towel around my body ready to head back to my room to get dressed for the day only to stop dead in my tracks when I see all of my clothes have been moved. It's not like I have much. I left pretty much everything I own back in Jackson, but to see my clothes hanging up next to Max's brings a sense of belonging. Unsure where my underthings are, I spy one of my bags on top of the dresser in the middle of the closet and open it to find what little bathroom accessories I have inside. Unsure where the rest of my things are, I start to open the drawers, and find my bras and underwear in the first drawer I open.

I pick a hot pink, matching lace set, a pair of jeans, and a long sleeve flowy top. I don't want to keep Max waiting, so I rush to put my lotion on and dry my hair as best as I can with a towel before I put on a coat of mascara and a swipe of lip gloss. I'm easy like that. I learned from my mom I don't need makeup. Only put on what will accentuate what you've got.

I find Max standing at his picture window in the living room, looking out with a thoughtful expression on his face.

"Are you already regretting having me move in?" I joke, but there's a ring of truth to it. I can't get over how easily he brought us into his house. There aren't many men who would do what he did.

He turns to look at me. His piercing blue eyes taking me in. "Not in a million years. I got the call that the dog doesn't have rabies."

My body deflates. I'd been praying that Beck and I wouldn't have to get rabies shots. I've been scared of needles since I read a book as a child with a giant needle and these soldiers that were inside. I'm pretty sure it was meant to make me feel better about getting shots, but it did the exact opposite.

I moved to stand beside him and look out the window at all the trees that surround his place. It's like living in a treehouse, almost.

"I found my things in your closet. Why didn't you bring my toiletries into the bathroom?"

Dipping down, Max takes my mouth in a short, but hot as hell kiss that leaves me breathless. "I knew if I came in the bathroom, I'd get into the shower with you, so I left everything in the bag."

My hands trail down his chest and along the ridges of his stomach, through his t-shirt, and stop when I reach his jeans. "I wouldn't have minded the company."

"I'll remember that for next time. Now grab your phone and purse before you distract me anymore. If I didn't know better, I'd swear you're averse to dates."

"To tell you the truth, I can't even remember the last one I went on. It's been years."

"Then I'm going to make up for all the dates you should have been taken on. How do you feel about Chinese?"

"Like I should have put on my sweatpants." I laugh. The only places I've eaten at since being in Murfreesboro are the shelter and the pizza place. I'm not a picky eater, but the thought of some Chinese food has my mouth watering.

"That's what I like to hear. It's a little hole in the wall that most people overlook, but it's the best Chinese in the state."

Linking my arm with his, I skip to his large steps out to the truck.

"And here I thought you didn't want to go on a date with me. I guess I should have mentioned Chinese first." He smirks at me from his side of the truck.

Reaching over, I pull his hand into my lap and play with his rough fingertips. "I'm sorry if I made you feel that way. It was never my intention. I do want this date, but I didn't want you to feel obligated either."

Max pulls his fingers free from my grip and wraps his hand around the side of my neck. Not hard, but enough to get my attention. "Listen to me. I don't do anything I don't want to do. It's as simple as that. And I don't want you to do something you don't want to do just to appease me either. Just be honest with me. It's as simple as that."

"I'm sorry. It wasn't until I left my old life behind that I realized how much I'd changed. If you can believe it, I used to be a strong, opinionated girl, but she slowly started to slip away sometime after I had Beck and then withered out of existence once Bradley was in my life." I swallow down the emotion that threatens to take over. "I've never met a man like you, Max Black. Since I started dating, men have always wanted one thing from me, and played games with me to get it."

"Boys can be assholes when they don't mean to be. In

high school, all we can do is think with our dicks. There should be a class on it they make girls take so they know what they're up against, but I'm no boy."

He certainly isn't. Max Black is all man. And it seems he's all mine as well.

Max is right. When he pulls up to the Chinese restaurant, it's a place I'd never look at twice. It's close to where he lives, so that must have been how he found it.

We step inside and there are only three tables with chairs around them, but the line to order is twenty deep.

Max stands behind me and wraps his arms around my waist. I feel his hot breath on the shell of my ear before he speaks. "I thought we'd order and then we can take our food to the park. Have a little picnic and enjoy the sunshine."

It really is a beautiful day. It's in the sixties; the sun is warming the slight breeze. I'm tempted to turn and look at him, but when I notice every set of eyes on us, I keep facing forward and read the menu.

I know it won't take long for everyone to know I'm with Max if they don't already know after the game yesterday. It didn't escape my notice that most of the moms were looking at me when I'd turn their way. It seems I'm the talk of the Little League team. I only hope it doesn't come to bite me in the ass if Bradley comes looking for me. There's no reason for him to come looking here, though. I have zero connections, and it was a random pick on where the buses were going that day. If I'd had more time to plan, I might have picked someplace else, but I'm glad I didn't.

Maybe it was fate that brought me to Murfreesboro and into Max's arms.

I dig my chopsticks into one of ten containers of food we have sitting around us and pick up a piece of Kung Pao shrimp before tossing it into my mouth.

"How do you do that?" Max chuckles from beside me. His long legs are stretched out as he leans on his arm. He's got a fork full of noodles hovering close to his mouth. "I've never been able to figure out how to eat with chopsticks."

"It's probably because my mom's favorite place to eat by their house is a Chinese place. Her and our neighbors used to get it at least once a week. We'd have a spread like this, but there were more of us to eat it. Me, my sister, Ava, and my sister's best friend, Birdie, just picked it up."

"Your parents are really great. I can't believe they want to buy a place here though." He shoves the noodles into his mouth and smiles at me.

"They are pretty great." I set my chopsticks in one of the containers and turn my body toward his and bite on the inside of my cheek. "Does it bother you that they want to buy a house here?"

He finishes chewing and sets his fork down to hold my

hand. "Not at all. Now, if they wanted to move into my house, I might not be up for it, but family's important. I want you to be able to have your parents here and for them to come to Beck's games and to watch the baby grow as much as they're able."

My eyes mist up at his words. He can't be as perfect as he seems. There has to be something wrong with Max; I just haven't found it yet.

"Plus, we can always visit them. I wouldn't mind some beach time every now and then." He looks down and when his gaze comes back up, his face turns serious. "Speaking of the baby. The hospital checked you out and everything, right?"

"Yeah, I didn't even know I was pregnant until that day. Talk about a shocker." My chest aches thinking about that night. Who knew something so devastating would bring me to where I am now? "They checked both of us out and said everything looked fine. Why?"

"I don't know much about pregnancies or babies. Literally next to nothing, but I want you to start seeing a doctor that's meant for that type of thing."

"An OB/GYN? I'm thinking of finding a midwife or a doula. I need someone who won't put me on the books." I cringe at what this means. "And that entails me giving birth not in a hospital." And with no pain meds.

Max's face hardens. "Beauty, I think it's time for you to tell me what you learned that night. The way you talk scares me and I'm pretty damn unshakable. I need to know what we're dealing with."

I know I should tell Max, but I don't want his life in danger. It's already bad enough we've started a life here. What happens when Bradley finds me? What will he do to the people I've grown to care about?

THIRTEEN
MAX

THE FEAR I see in her eyes has me scooping Delilah up and sitting her in my lap. "You can tell me anything. Nothing you say will change the way I feel about you. I only want to be better able to protect you. I don't even know what to look out for."

She lays her head on my shoulder and shudders. I hug her to me and give her time to tell me what I desperately need to know. I thought she'd tell her parents, but her dad came to me last night and asked if I knew what happened. The fear in his eyes had me vowing I'd do everything in my power to protect his daughter and grandchildren.

"When I first met Bradley, I didn't know who he was, and now thinking back on it, I think he wanted it that way. He said and did everything perfectly until we moved in. It was like a switch flipped and the man I thought I knew was gone." She takes a deep breath and holds it for so long I start to worry. Right as I'm about to pull her away and check on her, she blows it out. "It was an accident when I found out he was a lawyer on a political path. We were at some gala he said was for work, but when I was in the bathroom, I learned it was for his father, who is the governor of Mississippi."

That doesn't seem like a big deal, but I know there's more, so I keep quiet knowing how difficult it is for her to open up and tell me this information.

"Once I knew who his father was, I was curious why he didn't tell me. Then one day, I saw an article online saying how corrupt his dad is and his grandfather. He's a state representative in the House. I thought nothing of it, though. People hate politicians and make up lies every day. I was going to show the article to Bradley when he got home, only it was gone. Any mention of it was wiped off the internet. Who has the power to do that?"

Someone very big.

"He said I was tired and must have imagined it, but I knew I didn't. I went along with it but kept my eyes and ears peeled for anything else. There was this niggling feeling deep down in my gut telling me I needed to stay on my toes and not let it go. But the second I'd see something; it was gone in a matter of hours. It made me think maybe I was going crazy, and I was imagining it because I wanted to."

What kind of family was she involved with?

No wonder she's had such a hard time believing in me. This mother fucker tricked and deceived her at every turn.

"There were a few times I'd overhear him on the phone, but the second he knew I was anywhere near he'd get off. It was then I started looking for cameras in the house because how would he know where I was. The one's I did find wouldn't explain how he knew of my location in those moments."

She looks up and cups my face. "Are you sure you want to know?" I nod, needing to know everything. "Because once you do, there's no going back. I feel like I've already put your life and the lives of the people you love in danger by staying here and getting close to you."

I want to tell her she's among the ones that I love, but now isn't the time. She needs to get this off her chest. Plus, if she only knew of the trouble the women and men in the Mayson family had been in, she might think differently.

"I need to know everything. Don't worry about me. I can take care of myself."

"I hope you're right. The night everything happened, Bradley came home, and he was angrier than I'd ever seen anyone in my life. He stormed through the house and went into his office and slammed the door shut. At first, my natural inclination was to stay away, but after hearing him on and off the phone for two hours yelling, I had to know what was going on. When I looked for cameras, I never saw any leading to his office, but now I know he must have had one put in otherwise he never would have known I was outside his door."

I smooth my hand down her back and hold her close. "It's not your fault he's a bad man. I'm just happy you and Beckham are away from him now."

"I don't know it all, but what I know is enough to get his entire family put in prison. From what I gathered, Bradley has a drug business on the side. That's bad enough, but they've been smuggling women in and out of the border with drugs. Women that have been sold to them by others who couldn't pay off their debts. One of the women died at the airport and I don't know how, but she had something that would lead authorities back to the Stanton family if they found it."

Delilah looks around the park and when her eyes come back to me, she has tears streaming down her face. "He… ordered…" She hiccups and starts to cry in earnest now. "He ordered them all to be killed."

Hugging her to me, I cradle her to my chest. "It's okay, beauty. I'm here and won't let him hurt you ever again."

"That's what scares me."

My brows furrow. "What's that?"

"That you'll do something to protect me and get yourself hurt or killed."

"Now that I know who we're dealing with, we need to be more vigilant about making sure our surroundings are more secure. I'll talk to Cobi who's a police officer and see what he suggests." She looks up at me with wide eyes. Her cheeks are pink and wet with tears. "I won't give him specifics, but enough for them to advise me on what I need to do to keep everyone safe."

She tries to wipe the tears away, but more follow. "He'll probably tell you to dump the dead weight and pretend like you never knew me."

"That's not ever going to happen. Do you hear me? You're mine now and I'm not going to let some sketchy, lying, murdering bastard take you away from me."

"I should have left sooner." She nuzzles her face into my neck and whimpers. "I think as things escalated, that's when he started to keep me more and more isolated from the world. He never planned on me finding out."

Likely until she was a casualty.

"He knows what I know, and he's not going to stop looking for me."

Unfortunately, she's more than likely right. It hasn't been that long. Only a matter of weeks.

"Maybe as time goes on and he realizes you're not going to do anything with the information, he'll forget about you and move on." Even as I say the words, I know they're only to make us both feel better. Delilah's right. He'll likely never stop keeping an eye out for her.

I flip the ends of her hair, and it makes me want to see what she looked like as a blonde because I know I won't be able to see her natural hair color until she's safe from them.

Hugging her tighter, I kiss the top of her head. "Thank you for telling me. You did the right thing. I only hope now I can make it easier for you. I'll ask around to see if we can find someone who will keep you and the baby off the books."

She nods into my chest and when she speaks her voice is muttered, but I can still make it out. "Is this too much for you?"

I pull her back so she can see the truth in my eyes when I tell her. "Not even a murdering ex-boyfriend is going to keep me away."

"You, Max Black, might be crazy." She smiles and sniffs.

Never did I think I'd be in this position or find my person like my dad did, but now that I've found her, there's nothing and no one who will take her away from me.

FOURTEEN
MAX

THE SECOND we pull into the garage, Delilah's parents pull up in their rental car. They've got big smiles on their faces while I can't hide the frown marring my own. I thought I'd have a little more time with Delilah before the house was full again.

"Mama," Beck hops out of the car and runs straight for his mom. "Did you know GiGi and PopPop are going to buy a house here?"

"I did." She squats down so she can hug and kiss him. "Isn't that exciting?"

He nods and runs back to her parents and grabs their hands to drag them into the garage.

"I'm guessing it was a successful outing going by your happy faces," Delilah states looking back and forth between all of them.

"It was." Her dad puts his arm around Delilah's shoulder. "We found a place not too far away from here. We figure if we're going to have a place here, we'd like for it to be a little secluded."

Lexie's face scrunches up with worry. "I hope that's okay, we won't be too close?"

"Of course, not. What's the point of you living here if you're going to be far away again?" Delilah says with a big grin on her face. Her parents being here makes her happy, which in turn makes me happy.

"I promise we're not the type of neighbors who just pop in unannounced." Lexie blushes as she speaks.

"We learned that lesson the hard way when we walked in on our neighbors going at it in their living room. After that, we thought it would be best to call or knock so…" Ryder trails off.

Yeah, I'm sure her dad doesn't want to think about his daughter having sex with me or anyone for that matter, and definitely doesn't want to see it.

"A call would be good, Daddy," Delilah says softly. "Anyway," she says and turns to move inside the house, "did you guys have lunch? We picked up some Chinese and had a nice picnic at the park, but if you're hungry, I can—"

"We're good, sweetheart. We ate while we were out. Did you have a nice date?" Her mom arches her brow with a knowing look.

Delilah smiles and I swear it lights up the entire world. "It was probably the nicest date I've ever been on."

"That's because you were with shit guys before who didn't know how to treat you right," Ryder grumbles.

I'm going to take that as he likes me and knows I'll treat his daughter the way she should be treated.

Turning to look over her shoulder, Delilah asks. "What's that, Daddy?"

"Nothing, sweetheart. I'm glad you had a good time. It's about time someone treats you right for a change."

We all head into the kitchen, even though no one's hungry. It seems to be where we congregate the most. There and the living room.

Wrapping my arms around her middle, I lean down and speak quietly enough for only her to hear. The only problem is, once her ass is pressed into my hips, I have a hard time keeping my dick from trying to stand at attention. I think about what she told me earlier about what she went through, and it instantly deflates. "Hey, do you mind if I take Beck for a walk and talk to him about where you'll be sleeping from now on?"

She turns in my arms and scans my face for a moment before answering. "Yeah, sure, okay. I think it would be good coming from you."

It makes me happy that she trusts me with her son since I know how important he is to her.

"And later, I'll talk to your dad about Bradley."

Her face tightens for a moment, but I know it's not from me wanting to tell her dad. She's been dreading telling him everything that went down, and I think it would be best coming from me. If she saw how I think he's going to react, it would hurt her.

Reaching up on her toes, she kisses my cheek. "Thank you. Maybe later I can repay you."

"I'm not doing it for you to owe me, but if later you want to show me how nice your lips can wrap around my cock, I wouldn't oppose."

"Max," she scolds and looks around the room to find that her parents have moved to the living room. They're by the window, pointing at something.

My body shakes with silent laughter and I hug her to me. "I wouldn't have said that with them in the room. What kind of brute do you take me for?"

"One who can't control himself." She laughs into my chest.

She's right. It's hard for me to control myself around her when others are around, but I've managed so far.

"What are you going to do while I take Beck out?" I kiss her red, pouty lips.

"I think I'm going to lay down and try to take a nap." I'm close to asking her if she's okay when she answers for me. "I'm tired, but also a little nauseous."

"Go do what you need to do to feel better. Do you want some crackers and some ginger ale? I can bring some up to you before I go."

After the first time she felt sick, I asked my mom what to

do, and she sent me a list of things that might help Delilah when she isn't feeling her best. There's even some essential oil roller stick thing to help fight the nausea. It helps mostly, but I can see the tension in her eyes letting me know she's feeling worse than she's letting on.

"Um... I... that would actually be nice. I'm not sure if I can eat any crackers, but maybe the ginger ale will help settle me. I'll also use that fancy diffuser you got me and make that anti-nausea concoction."

"Sounds like a plan. I'll be up in a few minutes." I kiss her forehead and then watch as she takes the stairs slowly.

"Is she okay?" Lexie asks the moment her daughter is out of view.

"She's tired and feeling a little sick. I'm going to bring up some stuff to hopefully make her feel better," I answer, still looking up the stairs. "I'm going to take Beck for a walk after that and see how he's feeling about living here."

"Hmm," she hums. "I think there's more to it than that." The humor in her voice isn't lost on me. I turn and smile down at her. She's a little thing, just like her daughter. They look so much alike except for the hair color.

"I told Delilah I want her to be in my bed from now on, and she's worried about what Beck will think, so I thought I'd feel him out. See if he has any questions about his new living arrangement."

Lexie places her hand on my arm and gives it a pat. "I think that's smart. Make him feel involved. I know he doesn't act like it, but he's been through a lot. Delilah is his whole world, and while I don't know how much he saw or knows, he senses it."

"He's such a good kid it's sometimes easy to forget what he's been through."

"It is, but the good thing is he bounces back quickly. You talking to him and including him will go a long way. He adored you before he even met you, and now… I don't think you'll have anything to worry about with him."

With a quirked brow, I ask. "And do I need to worry about you and Ryder?"

"Not from me, but maybe don't announce to my husband you're taking his daughter to bed," she giggles. "While he's open to just about everything, there's only so much you want to know."

"Got ya. I didn't plan on it. I know Delilah's worried though."

"She doesn't need to be, and we'll be out of your hair soon enough. I'm going to look at flights while she's laying down and you're out with Beck."

"Are you leaving so soon?" I know Delilah will miss them when they're gone.

"Yes, but we'll be back." Lexie grins. "I have a job I need to do, and we need to buy some furniture for the house we want here."

"Did you put in an offer already?"

"We did, and the realtor thought they'd be very receptive

to our price, so we'll see." She shrugs. "Now that my daughter isn't in the room, tell me the truth. Do you care if we're just down the road, even if it is for only parts of the year?"

"As long as you call or knock when you come by, I don't think we'll have a problem." I smirk. "Really though, I don't mind. I know it will make both of them very happy to have you closer."

It isn't like we'll be able to have sex any time we want to. I won't be taking Delilah on the kitchen counter while Beck's awake. Now while he's asleep or at school is an entirely different situation altogether.

She pats my chest. "You're a good man, Max Black. Now, go take my daughter what she needs."

"Yes, ma'am." I chuckle.

"And don't call me ma'am." She walks away and speaks over her shoulder. "It makes me feel old."

I don't know how anyone would take Lexie for old. If I didn't know better, I'd think she's Delilah's sister. I can't wait to meet Ava and see how she adds to their dynamic.

Even though Delilah didn't think she could eat any more, I still pull out a sleeve of Saltine's for her to nibble on and a bottle of ginger ale. When I walk to her room, I'm shocked to not find her there. I keep walking down the hall to my room where I find her with her back turned to the door, and the comforter pulled up over her shoulders. While I'd been busy downstairs, she'd moved the diffuser I'd ordered for her into my bedroom, or I guess I should say our bedroom, and placed it on the nightstand. There are four little bottles of oil sitting by it. The room smells of citrus and peppermint. At first, when my mom suggested it I thought it would smell bad, but it's actually quite inviting.

I set down the crackers and her drink before I lean over and see she's already fallen asleep. Placing a kiss on her cheek, I close the door to the bedroom and then head for Beck's room. He's sitting on his bed with his baseball glove on his hand, throwing a ball into it.

"Hey, buddy. I thought I'd stop by and see if you want to go for a walk in the woods." I'm not sure if he'll take me up on my offer after getting bit by the dog out there. We've been hesitant to see, and with Lexie and Ryder showing up, they've been an excellent distraction from everything that happened that night.

He looks out his window and then back to me with worried eyes. "Is that dog going to be out there?"

"Nope, he's gone. If there's anything else out there that wants to hurt you though, it will have to get through me. So, what do you say we go outside and explore a little?"

He jumps off the bed and starts to put on his tennis shoes. "And maybe afterward we can play catch?" he asks, his entire face lighting up with hope at the question.

I ruffle his hair. His love for the sport is so refreshing compared to what I've become accustomed to over the years. By the end of my career, I was all about trying to make it through a game without thoroughly trashing my shoulder. Coaching the kids is bringing my love for baseball back to simpler times. "You read my mind, little dude. I'm glad I've got someone here to keep me in shape now that I'm not playing."

"Do you miss it?" he asks, looking up to me with curious eyes.

"I don't because I've got you and the team here, but maybe as time passes, I'll miss it."

He nods as if he understands exactly what I'm feeling.

Ryder and Lexie are nowhere to be seen downstairs when we step off the stairs, so we head out the back door. It doesn't take us long before we walk under the canopy of trees and follow the slightly worn path I've made from my outings since I moved in.

I hand Beck his water and ask. "Do you like it here?"

"Yeah." He nods. "What's not to like? I've never lived anywhere with so many trees."

"I like the trees too. It's one of the main reasons I bought the house." I'm not sure how to word what I want to ask him. I don't want to cause him any undue worry, so I give it my best shot. "How would you feel about living here permanently?"

He turns to me with his brows scrunched together. "I thought I already was."

"You are," I'm quick to say. "But I don't know how you feel about living with me."

"I don't want to leave. The man we used to live with wasn't nice to me when Mama wasn't around, and you're always nice to me. You like to play catch and you're teaching me about baseball."

The way he speaks is more mature than his seven years of life.

"Did your mom know he wasn't nice to you?" I ask, my temper flaring at the thought of anyone being mean to this boy.

"No," he hangs his head. "He… he said he'd hurt Mama if I told her, but he ended up hurting her, and I didn't say a word."

I stop dead in my tracks and bend until I'm eye to eye with him. Placing my hands on his shoulders, I clear the anger from my voice. "What Bradley did to your mom wasn't your fault. I know you didn't say anything and so does he, but Bradley is a very bad man."

One I'll all too happily end if he comes near either one of them ever again.

Tears well up in his eyes, making them even bluer. "Why did he hurt Mama?"

I can't tell him the truth, so I go with what I can say. "Because he's a bad man and didn't know what he had when he had it. I don't want you to think it was because of you because it wasn't, okay?"

"Okay," he answers but sounds unsure.

"You know I really like you and your mom. That's why I

brought you to my house to live. You're a smart kid, and I want to talk to you man to man. How would you feel if I was your mom's boyfriend?"

He purses his lips and looks to the sky, making me think he's about to say he doesn't like the idea. I hadn't thought about what I'd say or do if he actually didn't approve of us being together.

He finally looks down and when his eyes hit mine, I suck in a breath at the little man I see standing before me. "I know you'll treat her right."

"I promise I will."

I stand and start walking again. Beck runs to catch up to me. I'm quiet as I try to figure out how to talk to him about his mom sleeping in my bedroom now. I'm not sure how much he understands about boys and girls, and I realize I'm not as prepared for this talk as I thought. Maybe I should have waited for Delilah.

Beck points to birds and a few squirrels and rabbits he sees as we walk. When we come up to the end of the path I've made, I stop and look around us. We're about a mile from the house that you can't see through the thick trees.

"How would you feel if your mom and I shared a bedroom together and turned the one where she's been sleeping into a playroom for you? We can put in a TV and maybe a game system, a ping pong table, or whatever you like."

Closing my eyes, I groan. I can't believe I pretty much

just bribed the kid so his mom can sleep with me each night. That's how desperate I am to have her in my bed every night. Delilah is not going to be happy with me once she learns what just spilled out of my mouth. I don't even know how she feels about video games.

He turns his big blue eyes to me and asks so innocently. "Does she want to sleep with you?"

"Yeah, buddy, I think she does, and I want to sleep with her too. She's a great cuddler."

He nods in agreement. "Only if she wants to. Can we go play catch now?"

"Sure, buddy."

Now I just have to make sure I don't piss off the woman I want in my bed by bribing her son.

FIFTEEN
DELILAH

I STAND by Max's truck and watch as he talks angrily to one of December's cousins or nephews. I'm not sure which. There are so many in her family it's hard to keep up with all of them. I haven't even met half of them.

Whoever this guy is, he was waiting for Max when practice got over to speak to him. The second Max dismissed the boys, he went straight to Max and they've been talking ever since.

"Hey," December waves as she leaves school. "What's going on with Max and Cobi?"

I take my eyes off the two men to look at her. "Your guess is as good as mine."

"If I had to guess, it has something to do with you. Max wouldn't tell me what kind of trouble you're in. He said it was for my safety, but I know he's been worried about you and Beck." December smiles, looking off at Max and then at me again. "You know, I knew Max would be like his daddy when he found the right woman; he'd fall hard. I was worried there for a little bit he'd given up and was going to be a playboy for the rest of his life." A grin spreads across her face. "That was until he saw you for the first time. I knew right then and there, you are his one."

"Gareth was the same way?" It would help me feel more settled if I knew it's common among the Black men.

"Oh, yes, I didn't see him coming, but we fell hard and fast. Don't be like my sisters and fight it. It's so much easier if you don't, and in the end, you'll wish you had given in earlier."

Leaning in, I speak quietly even though there's no one around to hear us. "Even if there was a possibility of him getting hurt?" It feels like I've stepped into a dream after being alone for so long, and I don't want to lose this new family I've come upon.

"You can't think like that. He knows what he's getting into, and he knows how and what to do in order to protect all of you. Now, smile and wave so he won't worry."

When I look over, I see both men looking over at us. Cobi is frowning while I can't read the expression on Max's face.

"I should probably see what has him looking like that. Thank you for talking to me. I'm sure it probably doesn't seem like it, but it helps to know why Max is so gung-ho."

She pats my arm and gives a wave to the kids. "Happy to

help. If I don't see you before, I'll see you on Saturday at the game."

"See you soon." I wave goodbye and then walk to where the kids are playing around. "Beck, I'm going to talk to your coach, and then we'll be leaving, okay?"

Beckham's forehead puckers. "Sure, Mom."

I'm ninety-nine-point-nine percent sure everyone knows there's something going on with Max and me since we've been showing up to every practice and game with him since the night he picked us up outside the shelter, but I don't want to be the talk of the town, so I play it off.

Needing to see what's going on, I make my way over to Max. Long gone is the upset face, and now they're both laughing. I step up to them and the one December said was Cobi shakes his head at me.

"Delilah, I want to introduce you to Cobi. Cobi, this beautiful woman here is Delilah."

"It's nice to meet you," we both say at the same time while laughing.

Still laughing, Cobi says to me. "You're fooling no one with that… whatever that was." He slaps Max on the shoulder. "It's getting late, so I should get home to Hadley."

"I'll talk to you soon." Max gives Cobi a serious look. "Keep me updated."

"You'll know as soon as I know anything. Don't worry, man. We've got you." Cobi turns to me. "It's nice to put a face to the name."

"Likewise." I smile back.

The moment Cobi's out of hearing distance, I turn on him. "What was that about? It looked serious."

Max's lips turn into a thin line. "It is, but let's discuss it at home after Beckgoes to bed."

That only makes me worry more.

"Is everything okay?" I ask, wanting anything that will help settle my nerves.

Putting his arm around my shoulders, Max hugs me to him. "Come on, let's get out of here."

Panic swells in my belly, and claws up my throat, rendering me unable to talk. I can barely move my feet in the direction Max is leading me. He doesn't seem to notice how my entire body is shaking. Or at least that's what I think until he stops about ten feet away from the boys and turns to me. His hands go to my shoulders as he bends at the knees until we're eye to eye.

"Relax. Everything's going to be fine. Your and Beck are safe, but if you keep shaking like that Beck's going to sense something's wrong, and then he's going to get upset. You don't want that, do you?"

Of course, I don't. I'd never want Beck to feel the same way I do right now. Instead of answering, I shake my head.

"Alright then. Let's get Beck and pick up some Chinese." Leaning in, he kisses my forehead.

I nod, knowing what I have to do, but ask, "Did they find me?"

"Not yet." Max's jaw ticks.

Not yet. Meaning they will. Even now, Max knows it's going to happen one day.

Standing to his full height, Max takes my hand in his and takes two steps before he stops and turns back to me. It's the first time he's held my hand in public if you don't count the park where no one was around, and it breaks through the panic and makes me feel giddy.

"Are you ashamed to be seen with me in public?"

"What?" I swear my jaw must have hit the ground at his question. "Of course, not. What would make you think that?"

His eyes dart toward where Kari is standing with her eyes on us. "Because you act like I'm only your son's coach when we're out in public."

"You'll never just be Beck's coach. You're so much more than that and I'm sorry if I made you think that." It breaks my heart he'd think such a thing.

He dips down and brushes his nose to mine, his breath a whisper against my lips. "I want everyone to know you're mine."

I've given Max enough grief thinking we're moving too fast and thinking his feelings can't possibly be real. Believing in what December said, I go all in with this sweet beast of a man. "Then what are you waiting for? Show them I'm yours."

SIXTEEN
MAX

I LOOK through the report Cobi brought me for at least the tenth time, unsure of what to do. Someone has been asking questions about Delilah and Beckham, and I've got a good idea who it is. Who else but that asshole ex of hers would be looking for her? Her parents know exactly where she is. But do I keep Delilah and Beck inside and away from all eyes, or do I let them live their lives and worry about them every second of the day?

Small hands are placed lightly on my shoulders before Delilah dips down and kisses my cheek. "Is everything okay?"

Setting down the papers, I pull her down onto my lap and wrap my arms around her tiny waist. "Someone's still asking around about you and Beck."

All the blood drains from her face and tears threaten to spill down her cheeks. I hear the gulp rather than see it before she says, "I hate to say it, but maybe Beck and I need to leave."

"You're not going anywhere without me, so don't even think about it," I growl out. "Beck has to go to school, but I'm thinking *you* should stay home. I can take him to and from school and practice."

Her bottom lip trembles as she asks, "What if they recognize him while he's at school?"

She's right. Either I tell December what's going on or Beck gets homeschooled until we know they've moved on.

"I don't have all the answers, beauty, but I'm trying to figure out how to keep you out of harm's way. What I do know is you're not leaving Murfreesboro."

"What if I'm never safe? I don't want to have to look over my shoulder for the rest of my life." This time when she blinks, a tear falls down her cheek, but she hastily wipes it away.

"And you shouldn't have to. Why don't you stay here while I take Beck to your parents? I can update your dad so he's apprised of the situation and I can hear what he thinks we should do."

She sits up a little more in my lap. "I thought we were going out for dinner?"

"Maybe it's best if I pick up some takeout. We can sit out on the deck and turn on the lights you put up with the heater going." Then I can have her all to myself which is something I don't get too often. Plus, I can't do inappropriate things to her while we're out in public.

One night while we were sitting out on the deck when I had Delilah curled up next to me with a blanket covering us to keep out the chill, she suggested putting up twinkling lights in the trees closest to the house and along the deck. I was happy she was starting to see this place as somewhere permanent she'd like to decorate, so I gave her the go ahead.

She'd spent long hours skillfully arranging the lights to not be intrusive, but an accent to the night when we were outside.

"Yeah, okay," she says. Deflated, and starts to move off my lap.

I clamp my hands around her waist and keep her right where I want her. "Hey, it won't be forever, but for right now we have to do everything we can to keep all of you safe. Let me think about what options we have, but for now, staying home is the best option I can give you."

"You're right. Please don't think I'm not grateful for all that you've done because I know you do more than you tell me. It would kill me if something happened to you or anyone in your family for having any involvement with me."

She slumps against me and I know this can't be easy for her. She left one horrible situation to now feel imprisoned here. "I'm tired. I think I'm going to go tell Beck goodbye and then take a nap until you get back."

She moves to crawl off my lap again, but I hold her in place and bring her mouth to mine to get a taste of her. Only then do I let her go. "If you're still asleep when I get home, I'll come wake you."

Trudging up the stairs, she looks back when she reaches the landing with a sad smile on her face. Maybe I should take them to some exotic country until this passes over? I don't know the right answer, but I hate to see her like this.

Since it's not time for Beck to go over to his grandparents' house yet, I pull out my phone as I make my way into my office. I don't go in here often because I don't have much use for it, but I don't want my conversation overheard by Beck if he comes down.

My dad answers on the second ring sounding distracted. "Hello?"

"Hey, Dad. It's me. Are you busy?" I sit down in my leather chair and turn it until I'm facing the window so I can see out back.

"You know I always have time for you. What's wrong, Son?"

"How did you know something's wrong?" I ask curiously.

"Because I know you better than you know yourself. I can hear it in your voice." I hear the back door slide open and then shut. "Give it to me."

For the next few minutes, I tell him everything I've

learned since I last spoke to him about the situation with Delilah and Beck. "What do I do?"

He lets out a sigh. "Is there something in the water here that brings trouble to any couple the second they fall for each other?"

"There might be," I say, cracking a smile. "Murfreesboro sure has itself quite a bit of trouble when involving the Mayson clan."

"If you want to stay by her side—"

"Of course, I do," I say, cutting him off.

"Alright then, your options are to keep them in the house or go somewhere else. Both I know you don't want to do."

He's correct about that.

"They need to be caught and put in prison for the rest of their lives, so Delilah can live free and clear of their wrath," I growl down the line.

"That they do, Son, but you're not going to be the one doing it. You've got a woman now, a little boy, and a kid on the way." He chuckles. "Never in my wildest dreams did I think you'd be the reversal of me."

What the hell is he talking about?

"How's that?" I ask and turn in my chair when I hear some noise in the kitchen. Unfortunately, from my vantage point, I can't see in there.

"When I met December, I was single with two boys, and here you are finding your woman and you're inheriting two kids."

"Yours and mom's relationship definitely helped pave the way for me. It's taken Delilah some time to come to terms with the fact that I don't care that Beck and the baby aren't mine. One day they will be though."

"That's what I like to hear. I'm sorry I can't be of more help to you."

"It's a good thing you can't. If you could, it would probably mean you'd have a lot of trouble on your end. You've had enough to last a lifetime with my mom. I was thinking of getting a dog who could help guard the house, but I'm not sure if Beck is ready for that after the attack."

"It's not a bad idea. Why don't you ask him, and if he doesn't seem opposed, let him pick out the dog," he answers wisely.

"That's a good idea. I should probably go. I can hear the little guy now. I'll mention it to him when I take him over to see Ryder and Lexie."

"You know if you ever want me and Mom to watch him, we'd be more than happy to. I know it seems like you've got plenty of time right now before the baby comes, but in a matter of months there's going to be a baby who will need you both all hours of the day and night."

"We'll take you up on that offer, and soon. Will you also take a dog for a night?" I stand then and open the door to my office to see Beck bouncing around in the kitchen with his polar bear.

"I'm not potty training no dog, but I'll watch one for a night," he huffs down the line.

"When I know a date, I'll let you know."

"And keep me informed on what's going on. If you want, I can talk to your mom and see what she says about homeschooling Beck for a little while until you feel it's safer."

"If I take him out of school that means no more baseball too, and it would break that kid's heart."

"Better to break his heart than for him to get hurt, or worse," he states.

"I think if Delilah stays away from practice and the games, he should be safe, but I'll talk to her and see what she thinks. What we do know is they're looking for her."

"Don't think they won't use that boy to get to her. If they find him, they know she'll do whatever she has to do to save him."

Fuck if he isn't right.

"I guess it's a good thing the season's over next weekend. I was thinking of having the kids continue to practice until summer. Maybe I can get a couple of guys together to make a makeshift field on the back of the property."

"Did you ever think you'd meet someone who would turn your life upside down, but in a good way?"

"Never." I laugh. "But I'm glad I did."

"Me too, Son. Me too. And if you need help with your field, let me know. I'd be happy to lend a hand."

"Thanks, Dad," I say before I tell him goodbye. I walk

into the kitchen where Beck is still playing with his polar bear.

"Hey, buddy. Are you ready to go see your GiGi and PopPop?" He nods and keeps playing. "Do you have your bag to take for the night?"

"Oh, let me go grab it." He runs out of the kitchen and up the stairs.

I chuckle and watch as it sounds like a herd of elephants are stampeding through the house even though it's just his little body that's filled with excitement. He's only in his room for a second before he's coming back down the stairs with a smile, his backpack slung over his shoulder, and his bear in his hand.

"Ready?" I ask as I start for the garage.

"Yeah," he nods. "Do you think Mom will be alright here by herself?"

His question takes me off guard, making me wonder if he overheard anything earlier, because why else would Delilah not be okay?

"She'll be fine. After I drop you off, I'm going to get us some dinner, and then I'll be here with her." I scan his face to see if my words appease him.

"Some days she doesn't feel good, but she tries to pretend like she's not sick," he states.

"Growing a baby inside of you is serious business and some days are hard on her and makes her feel sick, but today I think she's only tired. The baby makes her tired too."

"You promise to take care of her?" he asks like up until now he's been taking care of her, and maybe he's felt that way. He is the best damn kid I know and if I have to build a whole baseball stadium on my land so he can play and be safe, I'll do it. I'd do just about anything for him and his mom.

I open the back door to my truck for him to crawl in and wait until he's firmly seated and has his seatbelt on. "I promise to always take care of you, your mom, and the baby. You don't need to worry about that."

"I knew I could count on you," he says.

And damn if his words don't make my eyes get a little misty.

SEVENTEEN
MAX

IT'S TWO HOURS LATER, and I thought for sure Delilah would be up from her nap when I got home, but as I look around the downstairs area, she's nowhere to be seen. For an instant, I get worried that while I was gone, her ex found her, but then I hear the strains of soft music coming from upstairs.

Setting down the takeout I picked up on the way home, I head upstairs wondering what she's doing. I wanted to get back sooner, but when I gave over the file I'm slowly amassing on Bradley Stanton the first, second, and third to her dad, he wanted to go over everything with me.

The bedroom door is closed when I get to the master bedroom, and it's quiet except for the light music. "Beauty?" I call as I open the door.

Stepping into the room, I take in the sight before me.

Delilah has on a tiny black scrap of lace covering her luscious tits and nothing else.

"I thought I'd welcome you home a little differently." She chews on her bottom lip as if she doesn't know she's the most breathtaking woman on the planet.

My dick salutes her and begs to be let out of the confines of my jeans.

"A man could get used to coming home to this," I growl and rip my t-shirt over my head as I start to prowl toward the bed.

"So, you like?" she questions, getting up on her knees where I can see her glistening pussy waiting for me.

"I more than like, beauty. I love. I guess you're not hungry if this is how you're greeting me."

"I'm hungry for one thing and one thing only, and that's you. Take off your pants and let me taste you." She curls her finger in a come-hither gesture.

I give her what she wants. Pulling off my shoes and then my pants, I grab my boxers by the waistband and tug them down my thighs, letting my cock that's hardening at a maddening pace free to slap against my stomach and then point directly at her. He wants her just as badly as I do.

The second my thighs hit the edge of the bed, Delilah reaches out and wraps both hands around my length. Dipping down, she swipes her tongue across my slit and then sucks my mushroom head into her wet mouth. I shudder at her touch.

Brushing her hair out of the way, so I can watch as she works me up, I pull it back and keep my grip on the makeshift ponytail.

Opening her mouth wider, she takes me in until I hit the back of her throat. I can't help but groan. It's hot as fuck when she tries to swallow my cock down her throat. Her pillowy lips stretch around my length. The sight before me nearly has me spilling my load, but I grit my teeth and hold off, enjoying the moment.

What's even hotter is how turned on she gets as she bobs up and down my length. Rubbing her thighs together, Delilah squirms and moans.

"Touch yourself as if it was me touching you," I say and then let out a long groan as she spreads her legs wide and slips her hand between them.

"Dip your fingers inside and give me a taste," I demand. If my cock wasn't halfway down her throat right now, I'd throw her down on the bed and bury my face between her legs.

Two fingers come up wet with her juices as she reaches her hand up to me. I dive and suck the sweet honey off her fingers until it's all gone and I'm dying for more.

Pulling my dick out of her mouth, I pick her up by the waist and crash my mouth to hers. It's short and desperate, just the way I'm feeling for her in this moment.

When I pull back, I take her with me as I lay back on the

bed. "I want you to ride my face while you suck me off. Turn around and sit on my face."

She doesn't waste any time turning around in my arms. In an instant, her pretty pink pussy is hovering over my face. "What are you waiting for?"

She takes it as me wanting her mouth on me when it's the exact opposite. I want my mouth on her.

Licking her.

Sucking her.

Tasting her sweetness.

I pull her down by her hips and quickly arrange my hands so I can spread her lips wide open for me. I want every inch of her exposed to me. I use my thumbs to open her hood and then swirl my tongue around her clit as if my life depends on it.

Delilah starts to ride my face just the way I want her to. She moans and I feel saliva start to drip down my shaft and to my balls. Never one to waste, she takes my balls in one hand and massages them, coating them with her spit.

I'm close to blowing, but I want her to come with me. With two fingers, I start to pump in and out of her, making sure I hit her in the right spot with every stroke. It doesn't take her long before her walls start to flutter.

"Baby, I need you to come with me. Do you think you can do that?" My hips shoot up, chasing her mouth.

She nods and starts to bob faster. Her little hands pumping along with her mouth.

I feel myself start to swell, about to blow, and she finishes me off by sucking on my tip and ringing my crown with her tongue. I shoot off in her mouth, trying to keep my hips under control and not gag her as I come down her throat. I quicken my fingers and crook them as I suck hard on her nub.

Delilah lets out a scream that I swear shakes the house as she grinds down on my face and rides me harder and faster until she lays spent on top of me. Her face on my thigh as she pants and shakes.

Holy hell, what a way to come home.

I don't leave her like that for long. Picking her up, I cradle her in my arms as I walk us into the bathroom and turn on the shower.

She picks her head up and smiles sleepily at me. "Welcome home."

"Welcome home, indeed. How about we get cleaned up, then we have some dinner, and then I'll get you all dirtied up again?"

Her eyes light up at that. "I like the sound of that."

Sticking my hand in to see if the water is warm yet, I find it the perfect temperature and then step inside with her still in my arms.

She looks up at me with a shy smile. I know what she wants. She wants me to fuck her in the shower and what Delilah wants, Delilah gets. At least where my cock is concerned.

"Put me at your entrance if you want me to fuck you," I say as I nip along her jaw and down the column of her neck.

Not wasting any time, Delilah positions me at her opening and then slowly starts to slide down my shaft. The moment she's fully seated, I feel her walls flutter around me. I know it won't take much to bring her over the edge again.

Leaning back against the cool wall, I place one hand at her waist to help her move as I thrust up hard. She moans with each stroke of my cock and her nails dig into my shoulders.

She starts to bounce on my dick like a champion, and the sounds she's making could make a grown man blush. They only make me harder and spur me on to fuck her harder seeing how fast I can get her to come. Hell, I came only minutes ago and I'm already about to detonate again.

"Don't stop," she moans and slips her fingers over her stomach and down to where we're joined.

Fucking hell, watching her touch herself turns me on unlike anything I've ever encountered. "I'm not going to stop. Keep riding my dick like that."

I take her mouth as she lets out a wail and swallow down the sound. Feeling it all the way in the pit of my stomach. It's then my balls start to tingle, and I know I can't last any longer. I latch onto her neck and suck as I let go. Groaning into her soft, wet flesh.

Not wanting it to be over, I kiss and lick along the column of her neck. Sliding my dick in and out of her slowly as I run my hand down her back and up again. I don't stop until I've grown soft and slip out of her.

It's then I lower her to the ground. She lets her body slide against mine and like I'm a teenager, I get a semi.

Delilah squirts some of my body wash onto her hands and rubs them together. She starts with my shoulders and works her way down. She smirks up at me when she gets to my length.

"You know you're pretty impressive."

I let my head fall back, and she washes my cock and then moves to my balls. "And here I thought it was you who was the impressive one for getting me harder than I've ever been. I can't get enough of you."

"Hmm," she hums, and moves to squat down and run her hands over my thighs and calves. Holy hell, I never thought having someone bathe me could be so erotic. "I think we make a pretty impressive pair. Don't you?"

"Yes, ma'am, I do. Now, why don't you stand up, so I can wash your sexy body." Her eyes spark with lust. I've been reading about pregnant women and how horny they can get, and I'm grateful to be reaping the rewards. "First, I want to feed you before I make you come again, but after that why don't we see just how many times I can make you come before you pass out."

She stands quickly and hands me her body wash. I try to wash her fast, but the way she looks up at me as if she wants me to consume her has me nearly breaking and when I run my hand between her legs and find her slick, I hike her leg around the crook of my arm and fuck her with my fingers until she can no longer stand. Only then do we step out of the shower with me carrying her back into the bedroom and sitting her down on the bed.

"Let me find you something comfortable and warm to wear. It cooled off pretty quickly while I was gone." Instead of going to her side of the closet, I grab a sweatshirt of mine for her to wear and a pair of sweatpants for me. I pull out a pair of thick socks from one of the drawers and I find a pair of pajama pants that won't swallow her whole.

Delilah doesn't say a word as I dress her in my clothes. She smiles and hums softly as I maneuver her limp body while I dress her.

"Can you walk?" I ask as I bring her to stand. She nods but wraps her hand around my arm for support. With four orgasms, I'm surprised her legs aren't jelly. I walk us slowly down the stairs and straight to the back door. "Are you ready for dinner?" I ask as I flip on the lights she put up.

"I'm starved." She says it in a way I'm not sure if she's talking about food or me. Damn if she's not insatiable tonight.

"Good. I picked up some of the finest fried chicken, mashed potatoes, cornbread, and greens this side of the state line."

Delilah turns on the patio heater and curls up on the wicker couch she selected for us to sit on while we're out back. We have a whole set of furniture that's being delivered by the end of the month for out by the pool. I can't wait to have her naked in my pool.

"What are you thinking about?" She laughs, eyeing the tent I'm sporting in my sweatpants.

"I'm thinking about you out here at night under the light of the moon and stars, naked and in the pool."

"What's stopping us from doing that tonight?"

I shake my head and step inside to grab the food. When I come back outside, she's standing by the railing looking out at the dark pool.

"First, we need to heat the pool. Otherwise, we'd be lucky to last a minute in the frigid water. But now that I see you like the idea, I'll start warming it up tomorrow and by the end of the weekend, it should be ready for night visitors."

We're quiet for a few minutes as we get our food and start to eat. "Isn't this better than having to be all dressed up and around a bunch of people?"

"Yes," she groans around a bite of fried chicken and then wipes her mouth. "I do see its appeal. If we were out, I wouldn't be able to rub you through your sweatpants." Her hand moves to the semi that's still tenting my pants.

"We should never go out again." I thrust my hips up into her hand, wanting more. I hate to do it, but I remove her hand from my junk and kiss her fingertips. "Later," I say, biting down on the tip of one.

She clears her throat and squirms a little before she settles. "You were at my parents' house for a long time."

"Your dad and I talked about Bradley and what we think is best. I talked to my dad earlier about it as well. While I have guys trying to find anything they can on your ex and his family, it might take a while to take them down, because I do believe eventually, we'll find something, or they'll get caught." I clasp my hand around her knee and start to rub circles with my thumb. "In the meantime, since school and the Little League season are about to be over, I want the kids to continue to practice. So, I was thinking of making a makeshift place for them to come here and practice. We'd call it off for the summer, but once it gets cooler at the end of September or the beginning of October, we can start practice up again while it's nice. What do you think?"

"I think they'd love that. They all look up to you and I know Beck would practice year-round if he could. I'm not sure why you're asking me though. It's your house. You can do what you like."

I swear under my breath. I thought Delilah had started to come around to the idea this place is hers as well as mine.

I arch a brow at her. "Are you planning to live somewhere else?"

"No." She shakes her head and takes a bite of mashed potatoes.

"This place and everything in it is yours, mine, and

Beck's. Therefore, you have a say on whether or not you want a bunch of kids here a couple of times a week."

Her cheeks pink up slightly, but she nods. "I don't mind. It will be good for Beck. Where are you thinking? I'm not sure I'd want screaming kids around once the baby's here."

I hadn't thought about that. "I'll make sure it's far enough away the baby won't hear."

"Oh," Delilah jumps in her seat. Grabbing my hand, she places it on her stomach. "Do you feel that?"

I start to shake my head no, but then I feel… something. It's barely there, but I… feel it.

Looking at her with wonder, I splay my hand across her stomach. "Is that…"

"The baby just kicked." She presses down on my hand, but after that one little bump, I don't feel anything.

Some days it's hard to remember she's pregnant, but feeling that little thump makes it real. In a matter of months, there will be a tiny baby here.

"This is going to sound crazy, but I want you to put my name down on the birth certificate." I close my eyes. I hadn't meant to say that. I wanted to say I want to be this baby's dad, and it came out all wrong.

"Do you think it will help keep the Stanton's off us?" she asks wide eyed.

Yes, but that's not why I want my name on there. I can't explain it, but I want the right to call this child mine. One day, once I ask Delilah to marry me, hopefully, she'll agree to let me adopt Beckham.

"Are you opposed?" She shakes her head and starts to open her mouth, but I stop her, not wanting to wait. If changing their name could throw the Stanton's off their trail, I don't want to waste any time. "I want to adopt Beckham too."

"Do you know what you're asking? Beck's never had a father. If you do this, you can't back down."

"He's a great kid. I'd be honored to call him my son. Even if for some reason things don't work out between us, I'll always be there for him. Beck and the baby."

"He'd really like that." She chews on the inside of her cheek. "Thank you for dinner, Max. It was great. If you don't mind, I'm tired and want to go to bed."

I have a feeling I said something wrong. I thought she'd be happy with my commitment.

"Sure. I'll clean up everything and be up in a few minutes." I want to ask her what I've done wrong, but she's up and inside before I can say a word.

By the time I'm upstairs five minutes later, she's fallen asleep with her body at the edge of the bed with the covers up to her chin. I slide into bed and pull her against me until her back is to my chest.

I should have told her I loved her. I should have said I want to marry her. Instead, I realize I sounded like I don't believe in us.

EIGHTEEN
DELILAH

I'M glad today is the last game for Beck's Little League. This week I popped. One day you couldn't tell I was pregnant and the next BAM! Everything is happening so quickly. I'm showing and I'm uncomfortable as hell sitting in these bleachers as I cheer the team on in their last game of the season.

I should have brought some sort of cushion to sit on, but I had no idea I'd be miserable sitting here. For the last two months, I've been to almost every game without a problem. So of course, it has to be now when my sister is visiting, my parents are here, and all the moms are looking and whispering that I can't sit still for the life of me.

Standing, I stretch and start to make my way down the bleachers when I spot Ava following. I don't wait for her. I want to get away from prying ears before we talk.

Once on the grass, I move to the fence that separates the viewers from the field and clasp onto the metal fence.

Ava bumps her hip with mine. "What's going on?"

"I'm just trying to get comfortable. Today the bleachers aren't doing me any favors." I wrap my arm around her waist and lean my head on her shoulder. Ava got my dad's height. Where I'm five-foot-two, she's standing tall at five-foot-eleven. She's willowy and gorgeous. I'm surprised she hasn't been hit up to be a model yet.

"How are you?" I ask her.

"Happy to graduate and be done with school, but now I've got to get a real job and be an adult." She looks at me with a fake frown on her face that makes me laugh.

Pulling away I take her hand in mine wanting her to see the sincerity on my face. "You'll do great with whatever you decide to do. I know it. Thanks for coming for Beck's last game. I know he's excited you're here."

"I wish I could have come sooner, but school was kicking my ass. At least mom and dad have been here to see most of his games. I can't believe they bought a place here," she says quietly as if they'll hear her from the stands. "But I bet you've been enjoying the nights Beck has a sleepover there, huh?"

I look at Max and sigh. It comes out sounding so dreamy it makes me laugh. Never did I think I'd be in love the way I am with Max. I still haven't told him. With my hormones being all over the place lately, I want those three words to come out at the right time and not because my hormones dictate when I say them. I'm also second guessing myself after he mentioned we might not work out in the long run.

At least my kids will have a father.

Max is an honorable man, and I know he'll never let down Beck or the baby. Maybe he's pulling back after I've been hesitant.

"You've got it bad, big sister," Ava laughs.

"I know I do. When I left Bradley, I never thought my life would become this." I indicate the field, Max, and his family with us in the stands.

"As awful as your time with Bradley was, I think it was to prepare you for the wonderfulness that you were about to receive. You deserve to be happy. You and Jacob never had a chance to fall in love, and maybe that's why you settled for that asshole, Bradley. I don't know, but this right here is where you're meant to be."

I think so too.

I give her a side hug. "How did you get to be so smart?"

"I've always been smart; you just never realized it until now." She laughs, hugging me back.

"I'm sorry I've been MIA from your life these last few years. I know I can't make up for the time that's passed, but I'm going to do better." I've missed my mom, dad, and Ava so much, and it tears me apart inside knowing I should have stood up for myself and demanded they be in my life instead of hiding what was going on with Bradley. It happened so slowly I didn't realize it until it was too late, and I'd isolated myself so completely I couldn't see the light if it was right in front of my face.

"We missed the hell out of the both of you, but now that we know what was happening, we understand why you did what you did."

That still doesn't make it any easier.

Max yells for Trey to run to another base with his hands cupped to his mouth. The way his muscles move with that action alone has me rubbing my thighs together in anticipation of what he'll do to me later tonight.

With my parents and Ava in town, Beck is spending the next two nights with them before they head back to California. Mom and dad have work, and Ava will be searching for her first job and is thinking of moving into an apartment with Birdie, her best friend.

"You're one lucky lady to end up with Max Black." She sighs while staring at him.

Giving her wide eyes, I confess. "You know, when I met him, I didn't even know who he was."

Ava gasps at me. "How did you not know who one of the hottest baseball players to ever live is?"

"I'm talented that way. I still know very little about the sport. If Beck wasn't in it, I wouldn't bother to try to learn."

Although I do want to also learn for Max now. He finds it hilarious I know so little about what he's spent his life doing.

"Well, don't let your man hear you say that." She looks

down and then rests her hand on my baby bump. "I can't believe you're pregnant."

"Oh, believe me, I am, and I'm feeling every bit of it today." I lean in so only she can hear me. Even though we're feet away it would be just my luck someone would overhear me. "Did you see the way those moms were looking at me when I was eating my crackers?"

"Yeah, they're jealous ass bitches. You know they probably think it's Max's and wish they'd been the one to get pregnant with his child and land him."

My shoulders deflate as I take a peek over to where Max is standing by the boys. He's talking animatedly to them, and they're listening with rapt attention.

"What's wrong?" Ava rubs her hand over my back.

"I wish this baby was Max's. Right now, he says he's fine with it not being his, but what if he changes his mind?" I confess with tears welling up until I can't see Max any longer. I've heard so many stories where the man dumps the mom and the baby after a few sleepless nights claiming he can't do it and shouldn't have to since the baby isn't his.

Ava looks at me worriedly. "Has he given you any reason to think he'll change his mind?"

"Not at all. In fact, he wants to adopt Beck, and for me to put his name on the baby's birth certificate. How is he so perfect?"

"Because he's a good man, and he knows that family is

what you make of it. Someone doesn't have to be blood to be your family."

I hug my baby sister and think of how ironic it is she's the one giving me advice. "You're too smart for your own good."

"Listen, neither Beck nor this baby will be pining after their biological dads. Max is going to be that man, and he's going to be the best damn dad those two could possibly ever have. Let him have a chance before you already have him failing. Now smile because everyone is looking over here like I'm being mean and making you cry."

I give a half-ass smile that I know isn't very convincing before I turn back to the field. "I don't know how Max has put up with me when I've doubted this entire thing from the get-go."

"After what you've been through, anyone would have doubts."

Even as she says it, I know I shouldn't have doubts. I feel like I've been brainwashed. When something is going right, I should trust it.

I hastily wipe away the tears that have started to fall. "I love him, and I can't even tell him because I'm afraid he won't believe me when I say the words."

"I think you're being too hard on yourself and overthinking it. When this game is over, I want you to march up to him and tell him you love him. Get it out there and I'll bet you feel a thousand times better. Plus, I bet he'll be even more rewarding in bed once you get home."

"Oh, god," I slap at her and laugh. "I can't wait until you fall in love and you're a mess about it."

"Who said I'm ever falling in love? I haven't even had a real boyfriend yet."

Real? Has she had a fake boyfriend? What even is a fake boyfriend?

"And that's my fault. First, with dad being so overprotective of you so you don't wind up getting pregnant like I did, and well… I don't know why you didn't have one in college." My eyes widen as a thought comes to me. I blurt it out without thinking. "Are you a virgin?"

She puts her hands on her hips and looks down at me. There's a playful smirk on her face, so I know she's not mad at me. "And what if I am?"

"It doesn't matter to me, but if you are, I'd like to know why. Are you saving yourself for marriage? The right guy? Are you gay?" I ask in rapid fire succession.

"Wow, you really went for it. But, no, I'm not saving myself for marriage nor am I gay." She laughs.

"Hey," Dad's voice says from behind us before he wraps his arms around both our shoulders, "what are my two girls doing over here talking in whispers about?"

"Just me falling apart." I laugh.

My dad doesn't, however. He slips his arm off Ava and wraps me in a tight hug. "What's got you upset?"

"I'm being stupid, that's all. Ava already talked me down," I murmur into his chest.

"She was thinking Max might change his mind about Beck and the baby once it comes and reality sets in. I told her blood doesn't make a family, and he's going to love them no matter what," Ava says with pride in her voice.

"She's right, baby girl. I'd disagree with her if I thought for even a minute that man out there isn't head over heels for you, but I know he is. I see the way he looks at you and the way he's doing everything in his power to protect you. If that's not a devoted man, I don't know what is."

I jump when the metal fence tings, and Max is standing there with a worried look on his handsome but serious face. "Is everything okay? Are you feeling okay?"

"I'm fine just uncomfortable up on those bleachers today for some reason." I smile at him, loving that he came over to make sure I'm okay. "The boys are doing great."

Max chuckles and shakes his head. "We all know you have no clue about the game, but yes, they're doing well."

I shrug my shoulders because it's true. "I'm trying though." I giggle.

"I know." He smiles fondly down at me. "Would you two give us a second before I have to get back out there?"

"Sure," my dad says, wrapping his arm around Ava's shoulders and steering her away.

Max hooks one finger through the fence. It's not easy to hold hands this way, but I manage to get two fingers over his and my thumb underneath. "Now, what's really going on over here?"

I look down, hating that he can so easily read me. I don't want to tell him about how I don't understand how he so easily accepted me, Beck, and the baby as his own. He doesn't deserve my insecurities, so I go with my other problem.

"Some of the women and moms look at me like I got pregnant with your baby, so I could trap you. They don't know how far along I am, and I'm sure to anyone who sees us together or knows how long I've been around, they presume the baby's yours."

"That's fine with me. We know the truth and when this baby is born, I'll be the only father he or she will ever know." He takes his other hand and places it lower on the fence where my stomach is. "Are you excited that next week we'll finally find out what's growing inside you?"

I laugh at that. "You make it sound like it could be anything. Maybe it's a watermelon, or maybe it's an alien."

His lips quirk up. "Poor choice of words, but whatever it is, it's our baby. I'll love him or her just like I love its mom."

Sucking in a deep gasp, my breath gets caught in my chest. It takes several seconds before I can speak and when I do it comes out stuttered. "You love me?"

"I should have told you last night. I…I wanted to say things, but they came out wrong, and then you were upset."

I was upset, and I didn't want him to see me cry over the

words he said. I was awake when he came to bed and pulled me into him. Once I was in his arms, I fell asleep instantly.

"I'm sorry I left you outside. I was upset. If you would have led with loving me…" I stop and smile thinking about Max loving me.

"I should have started with that. If you need me to prove it to you, I'll show you later when we're alone." He winks.

"I don't need you to prove it to me." I press my body to the fence. "I've been waiting for the right moment to tell you, I feel the same, but I wanted you to believe me when I said the words."

Max's thumb caresses my cheek through the fence. "Why wouldn't I believe you?"

"Because I'm a hormonal mess." It comes out a mix between a laugh and a cry. "I didn't want to say it after sex because you might think I said it in some blissed-out state and didn't mean it."

"Let me stop your right there, beauty. You can say those three words to me anytime you want and each time you say them to me, I'll believe them. You can say them crying or after crying. During sex and after. Even when you're mad at me. I don't care when, but if you're feeling them, I want to hear them."

"Max," I cry, "I need to kiss you."

Even though we're in the worst position possible, he doesn't deny me. With a finger on each side of my face, Max positions his lips through the fence and kisses me in front of everyone. Even though it's awkward as fuck, it's the sweetest, hottest kiss ever.

The crowd cheers and claps and for a moment I think it's for the game until my brain clears from its lust induced fog and I realize they're clapping for us.

I pull away and I know my cheeks are as red as a cherry. I can feel the heat all the way to the tips of my ears. It's then I remember I still haven't said those three words to Max, and he deserves them more than any other man on the planet.

I push up onto my toes. My fingers curling around the metal fence and press a chaste kiss to his lips. When I break away, I make sure to catch his gaze as I say, "I love you, Max."

Pulling away so Max can get back to the game and out of the spotlight, I stop when he calls my name. When I turn around, he's right where I left him.

"I love you too, beauty."

We decide to have a date at home instead of going out. I'm tired, and I want to spend as much alone time with Max as I can before my parents have to leave. They both have quite a few jobs they've already committed to, and we won't see them for the next couple of months.

Max told me to go relax while he whipped us up some dinner, so I headed upstairs and soaked in his giant tub until

I was pruny. Only then did I get out and get ready for our date. Whatever he's cooking smells amazing from all the way upstairs and I can't wait to taste it.

Slipping on a light dress, I twist my hair into a braid, put on some mascara and a coat of lip gloss, and I'm ready.

Stepping outside the bedroom, I see light flickering from downstairs. The smell of whatever he's cooking hits me tenfold and my stomach growls, wanting whatever Max has made for us. As I walk down the stairs, I'm greeted by at least a hundred candles that are lit everywhere the eye can see.

Max hasn't noticed me yet, too engrossed in stirring something in a saucepan on the stove. At least I thought he hadn't, but when I'm only a few feet behind him, he extends his hand behind him. I take it. Feeling the rough pads on his fingers skate along my wrist as he pulls me against him. Flush to his back, I wrap my arms around him and lay my head between his shoulder blades.

Running my hands up from his abs to his pecs and back down again, I say. "Whatever you're making smells mouth-watering. I already know I want seconds."

"Good. I haven't made this in so long I was afraid I'd mess it up. It's almost done. I just have to add in the chicken and pasta to the sauce. Do you mind getting the bread out of the oven?" he asks as he moves to the side, so I can get into the oven.

"Not at all. You should have kept me down here to help instead of letting me indulge myself in a bath."

Opening the oven, I pull out the garlic bread and set it on a placeholder already set out on the counter.

Max moves back and kisses the top of my head. "Nope, tonight is all about you. I want to make you feel good after being uncomfortable for hours today while you watched the kids play. I'm getting a cushion to use for next season. Maybe I'll have some made for the team and we can sell them to all the parents."

"That's a perfect idea. We could even do t-shirts and hats," I add. "Are you sad the season is over?"

"A little bit. It's definitely shorter than I'm used to, but I'm thinking I'm going to see if the parents still want to have practice to keep the boys' skills up; maybe twice a week until it gets too hot."

"Afraid you'll get bored?"

"I could never get bored with you and Beck around, but I would like to find something to fill my time. I'm thinking of helping out now and then with Mayson Construction if they need help." He shrugs. "There's plenty to keep me busy if you want me out of your hair."

"Can't say that I do, but I'll let you know if I get tired of you." I laugh. I'm not sure I'll ever get tired of being around him. "Do you need me to do anything else?"

"Just sit your pretty ass down at the table and I'll bring

this over in just a minute." He pours the chicken and pasta in with the sauce and stirs it.

"What are we eating?" I ask once I sit at the table. It's then I notice a bouquet of flowers in the center of the table. There has to be at least two dozen roses. Max really went out of his way to make tonight about me when I should be making it about him.

"Chicken, pasta and mushrooms with a creamy Madeira sauce," he answers as he brings the large skillet to the table and places it in the middle between two lit candles and the beautiful flower centerpiece. He walks back to the kitchen and grabs the garlic bread and some fresh parmesan cheese.

"I had no idea you have this kind of culinary skill. You've been holding out on me," I joke as he serves us both the pasta.

"I didn't want you staying only for my cooking." He winks, putting a piece of garlic bread in each of our bowls.

"True." I take a bite and moan around my fork. Only once I chew my bite do I speak. "If I'd known you could cook like this, I might have made you my slave."

Covering my hand with his, he gives me a mischievous smile. "I'm already your slave, beauty. All you have to do is ask and I'll do anything you ask of me."

"I like the sound of that."

"And I like the sound of you eating my food. I'm not sure how long I'm going to be able to hold myself back from taking you right here on this table." He reaches down and adjusts himself.

"Is dessert you?" I ask before taking another bite and moaning.

"All I know is I'm having you for dessert. I'm going to lay you out on this table, dive my face between your legs, and not come up until your hoarse from screaming my name."

Yes, please.

"I see you like that idea." He chuckles darkly. "Don't worry. We've got all night to have fun, and I plan to ravish your body until you can't keep your eyes open."

There's nothing better than a man who takes immense pleasure in pleasing his woman, and Max does to the extreme. He knows exactly what I want and how to wring every last bit of pleasure from my body each time we're together.

"You've gone quiet," he says before taking a bite.

"I'm only thinking of how good you make me feel. Each time gets better and better with you. I wonder if it has anything to do with me being pregnant and the extra blood flow…" If it's all Max.

Max responds by winking. "Eat and I'll show you."

"I don't want to rush such an amazing meal." I try to keep a straight face. There's nothing that I want more than to give my body over to Max and his skills.

"I'll make it again. Whenever you want, just eat quicker."

I can't help but laugh at his impatience, even though I'm feeling the same way. Perhaps even more so. I can barely sit still on my chair. The need to feel Max inside of me is building with each passing second and it won't be long until I'm ready to combust.

"Am I eating too slow for you?" I ask, bring my fork to my mouth with intentional slowness.

"You're not going to think it's so funny when I spank your ass later for torturing me like this."

Like that's a punishment. "All good things come to those who wait."

"I've been waiting for you my entire life. I think the time for waiting is over."

Even as good as the dinner is he's made, I set my fork down before I stand up and move to position myself on his lap. I run my fingers through his hair that's starting to get a little long, but I love it. It gives me something to hold on to when he's driving me wild with his tongue. "You shouldn't have to wait a moment longer."

He places his hands on the table on either side of me and I think he's going to rip my dress off, but instead, he leans forward, running his tongue along my bottom lip as he moves all the dishes out of the way.

Picking me up by the waist, he sits me on top of the table. I can't stop watching as his hands slowly move up from my calves to my knees where his fingers disappear under the hem of my dress.

When I glance at Max, his eyes are locked onto where his hands just disappeared to. He must feel me watching him because he looks up and his blue eyes are dark with desire.

"Lean back and let me taste your sweet pussy." His voice is rough and thick with want.

I've barely leaned back on my elbows when he flips up the skirt of my dress and spreads my legs with his wide shoulders.

Dipping down he licks me from back to front and then swirls his tongue around my bundle of nerves giving it a jump start.

He rumbles his approval and then dives deep, spearing my core with his thick tongue. Lick after lick, he makes noises of approval. When his head pops up, he growls out, "You taste sweeter and sweeter every day. If it was possible, I'd keep you pregnant forever."

"What?" I want to argue but words halt on my tongue when two fingers plunge inside and start to pump, curling in the right spot while he fastens his lips around my clit and starts to suck.

Heat builds deep in my core. My toes curl. Reaching down, I tangle my fingers in his hair and hold Max right where I want him. It won't take much more before I fall over the edge.

One hand skates up my stomach and pulls down the fabric until my breasts break free. They fall out and pucker as the cool air hits the buds. In tandem, he swirls his tongue around my hardened nub and pinches my nipple.

I arch as pleasure takes over, shooting out of my pores as I groan and grind my core against his face.

Pumping slowly, he brings me down with small thrusts and little licks until I'm flat on my back, staring up at the ceiling, and trembling with aftershocks.

I hear Max and look down my body to find him pumping his shaft with slow strokes.

When did he lose his clothes?

"I love seeing your pussy wet and dripping for me. Now I'm going to fill you with my cum, so I can watch it drip out of you and coat your creamy thighs."

Fuck, how his dirty words turn me on.

He pumps in languid strokes as he stares at me. "I told you I wanted to show you I love you, but fuck if I don't want to bend you over this table knowing your succulent tits are pressed against the cool wood and smack that ass of yours until it's pink while my dick's inside of you."

"Yes," I answer breathily. "You show me with every action. Now I want you to take me how you want me. Make me come harder than I've ever come before."

"Fuck, you're perfect for me. Turnover and show me that perfect ass of yours, beauty."

I do as I'm told, pulling my dress up around my waist while my breasts press into the table and send a shiver through me. I feel the hairs on his thighs brush against the backs of my legs seconds before he runs one large hand down my spine and over my ass to dip inside. Wet fingers ring around my tight hole, smearing my juices around and putting pressure but not pressing inside.

"Do you want my fingers inside here while I fuck you?" He presses a little harder but doesn't breach my entrance.

I don't answer but press back, showing him what I want.

"Perfect," he says as he positions himself at my entrance and slides inside in one swift thrust.

Placing one hand at the small of my back, he pistons his hips. His pelvis slaps against my ass and then smack. I jump and moan, my walls spasming around his thick cock.

"I love feeling you squeeze me and pull me deeper," he moans. His fingertips dance over to the other cheek and circle once before I feel them leave my skin and then the sharp crack of his hand against my flesh.

I moan louder and stick my ass out for more.

"Your ass is a pretty shade of pink. I think I'll reward you with my fingers."

He slides his fingers through the wet that's gathered and pushes at the tight ring.

"Breath," he soothes.

I try to steady my breaths, but it's difficult when each thrust brings me closer and closer to where I want to be.

I relax my body as he slowly pushes a finger inside. I'm so full it's almost painful, but with each stroke, I stretch, and my body accommodates the intrusion. It doesn't take long until I'm panting with the need to come and thrust back in tandem with him.

"Tell me you love me," he demands. He leans over me, his hand moving around to grab me by my throat.

"I love you," I pant.

He thrusts faster and deeper and I feel him swell inside of me.

"Tell me you're close," he rumbles from right behind me.

"So close. I just n..." I don't finish because he pulls his hand from the small of my back and moves around my front to pinch my clit.

Fireworks explode behind my eyelids as I quake around his jerking cock. I fall flat against the table as I ride out the aftershocks and feel him still deep inside of me.

Gently he pulls out of me and picks me up, cradling me in his arms as he sits down on the edge of the table.

Kissing the side of my neck, Max breathes heavily. "Let me catch my breath and then I'll take you upstairs and make love to you for the rest of the night."

NINETEEN
DELILAH

"I'M GOING to go stretch my legs," I tell Max before I stand. I'm not sure how I let him talk me into coming to the town's high school football game. I was already uncomfortable at Beck's when I was five months pregnant, and now I'm rounding on nine months. No woman this pregnant should be sitting on the bleachers. Max has even brought me a cushion, but it isn't cutting it for me tonight.

The baby's kicking up a storm and playing a little football of her own with my organs as we sit here. Maybe if I stand it will give her a little more room, and she'll stop using my organs for practice.

Max stands too, helping me up. "Do you want me to come with you?"

"You hang out with your family. I won't be gone too long unless the bathroom line is exceptionally long." Because I pee every five minutes or so it seems, I have to use the nasty bathroom in the concession stand.

"If you're sure," he says, already sitting down and turning to the group of guys we're sitting with. Max has his brother, his dad, along with December's dad, Asher, all at the game. December and November are on their way and then I'll have someone to talk to that doesn't want to talk about sports I don't understand.

Hanging onto the banister, I waddle down the bleachers and sigh with relief once my feet hit the concrete of the sidewalk. Every time I walk down those damn bleachers, I feel like I'm going to fall flat on my face. It doesn't help that I'm stomach heavy, and my balance is off. Half the time, I feel like I could fall from how big my stomach is while in the house. These rickety stands aren't helping matters.

While I feel as big as a house, Max has made me feel beautiful every day. In fact, I think the bigger my stomach gets, the more turned on he is. It's some weird fetish that I don't want him to get accustomed to because I'm not sure I can handle another pregnancy. At least not for a long while.

Pulling out the keys to Max's truck, I click to unlock it, but it doesn't beep. I hit the button again and again, but nothing happens. The lights don't even flash.

I sigh and look to make sure I have the right set of keys. I've been driving around using Max's SUV that he's all but given me to use. He took out everything of his and deemed it my car one day. Surprisingly I didn't agrue. For once, I'm enjoying having someone take care of me.

But the keys in my hand are the right ones. What I'm not sure about is why they aren't working. I want to get inside and grab the lip gloss I left inside earlier. My lips feel dry, only adding to my uncomfortable state.

Pulling out my phone, I bring the screen to life to text Max and ask him if he knows what's wrong with his truck when my hand is hit, and my phone goes flying.

What the hell?

I turn to look at whoever just slapped my phone out of my hand when I'm cut short by the one person I never wanted to see again. It's dark in the parking lot and where we parked is even darker than some of the other spaces, but I'd know him anywhere. My body starts to tremble as Bradley rips my purse from my arm and crowds me into the side of Max's truck.

He leans in. His hot breath fans my face and I smell the stench of alcohol on his breath. He doesn't stop until his body is pinning me against the hard surface of the truck. "It's been a long time, D. Have you missed me?"

I shake my head, hoping this is all just some bad dream, and I'll wake up.

"That's too bad because I've missed you. I've missed these succulent tits, and your tight pussy." He looks down at me and sneers. "I guess it won't be tight for much longer."

I try to push him off me, but he doesn't budge. No,

instead he grabs both of my arms in a bruising hold and shakes me like a ragdoll.

"You should have stayed." He takes both my hands in one of his large ones and grabs me by the throat with the other. "Now I have to assume the worst. Did you tell your new friends about me and what you overheard?"

I try to shake my head no, but his hold is too tight. "No," I choke out. His hold on me becomes tighter, cutting off my airway.

"Somehow I don't believe you. Do you want to know why?"

No, I don't. All I want is for him to let me go and leave me alone, but I know he won't do it. Not now that he's found me. I knew this day would come, but I didn't think it would be today.

After it seemed like Bradley and his goons were no longer looking for me, we became complacent. I should have stayed home and never left the house.

"How did you find me?" I squeak out.

"It seems you've forgotten who I am. You can't hide from me. I'll always find you." He leans in and licks the side of my face, and I want to throw up when his dry tongue hits my skin. "This is new," he lets me go to grab my protruding stomach. "What I wonder is… is it mine or is it your famous baseball player boyfriend's?"

I cough and sputter until I catch my breath. When I can

finally breathe easy, I see his face twisted up. He's evil. There's no other word to describe what Bradley is.

My body goes slack at the knowledge he knows who Max is. "Please don't hurt him," I beg.

"Oh, I'm not going to lay a hand on him. Your little Beck is safe as well. I'm going to hurt them by hurting you." His eyes are dark and dilated as he grabs me again roughly by the arms and slams me back against the truck.

"I remember a time when you told me you didn't want any more kids." He laughs, and it's pure unadulterated evil. "Let me help you with that. If you make it out alive, we'll see if pretty boy Max Black still wants you." He leans in and bites down on my earlobe. "I have a confession. I don't think he'll want you after I'm through with you."

"What are you going to do?" I cry out as he drags me further into the parking lot. It's darker back here. Eerily dark. When he starts to pull me into the trees, that's when I start to fight. I can't let him take me where no one will see. He's going to kill me and if he doesn't, I'm sure I'll wish I was dead.

"I'm just going to rough up that pretty little face of yours." He grabs me by the face and squeezes hard enough I taste blood in my mouth. I know this isn't even the worst of it. "Maybe cut off this ugly hair of yours." He flips the ends of my hair and snarls at me. "Did you really think changing your hair color would deter me for long?"

"I just wanted a fresh start," I say with my mouth smashed together.

"Well, I'm about to give you a fresh start. When I'm done with you, no one will want you. Even Beck won't be able to look at you." Grabbing me by the throat again, he cocks his arm back and starts to laugh. "Tears won't save you. In fact, nothing will save you now."

I don't realize I'm crying until he smears my tears with this thumb and digs the pad into my lip until my flesh breaks and blood starts to trickle down my chin.

"You should have minded your own business, bitch." It's the last thing he says before his fist slams into my face. Pain explodes through my nose and eye to the point I can't see anything. I don't need to see to feel what he's doing to me, though.

Pulling me by the hair, Bradley drags me over the curb and throws me front first into a tree. Now on the ground, I try to curl into a ball to protect my baby, but he's too strong. He kicks me in the side and waits until I arch my back in pain for him to stomp down as hard as he can on my stomach.

One second there's pain, and the next everything is dark. There's no more pain. No more Bradley. No more anything.

TWENTY
MAX

"HEY," Mom hugs me and sits down beside me, "where's Delilah?"

Looking at my phone, I realize it's been almost half an hour since she left. There are no messages from her, though, making me wonder where she is.

"She was uncomfortable and went to stretch her legs." I think about her mentioning the bathroom. "Did you notice if the bathroom was busy or not on your way in?"

Mom and November both shake their heads. "I can go check to see if she's in there if you're worried," Mom says already standing.

"Would you? I thought she'd be back by now and her staying gone this long isn't like her."

She smiles down at me. "She's probably in line or getting some food."

I want her to be right but can't help the feeling that something is wrong.

Placing my hand on Mitchell's shoulder, I point to Beck. "Can you watch him? I'm going to go see what's holding Delilah up."

Mitchell, my dad, and Asher all nod in agreement. Good, I don't need to worry about Beck as well. I take the steps two at a time and by the time I round the bleachers I see Mom coming out of the bathroom with no Delilah insight.

"I didn't see her in there, and I asked if anyone had seen Delilah, but no one's seen her since the beginning of the game. I checked the concession line as well on the way. Do you have any idea where she'd be?"

I have no idea where Delilah could be if not in there.

"Why don't you go back and sit with Dad while I search for her. If you see her have Delilah text me or you text."

I start to step away when Mom's hand comes to my arm and there's a worried look plastered on her face when I turn back to her. "You don't think she's in trouble, do you?"

"I don't know," I tell her, but deep in my gut I know it's been too long and she's in trouble. Now I just have to find her.

"Go, go," she pushes me, her voice trembling, "go find her."

I start off walking quickly, but as I scan the area and don't find any sign of her, I start to jog through the parking lot. Up and down each row I look, but it's empty except for cars and trucks. By the time I've made it to the back row, I'm all but sprinting. Sweat is pouring down my face, and stinging my eyes, but I don't care. All I care about is finding Delilah.

Stopping, I rest my hands on my knees and try to catch my breath as I survey the area. I saw my truck, so I know she didn't take it for some reason. It's then that I see some movement out of the corner of my eye at the edge of the trees.

I take off running full out, trying to get there as fast as I can. There's a body on the ground and the closer I get, dread infiltrates me until my entire body feels like it's full of poison. "Delilah," I shout, falling to my knees when I reach her.

She doesn't respond. It's dark, so I can't see much, only that she's curled into herself. "Delilah, baby, are you okay?" I ask as I turn her onto her back.

A low moan comes out of her, making my worry escalate. I'm terrified of what I'm going to find as I pull out my phone and turn on the flashlight.

What I see has me gasping for breath. I feel sick, but I don't have time for that. Delilah needs me. Her face is bloody and swollen to the point that if I didn't know her and what she was wearing earlier, I wouldn't recognize her.

There are angry red marks and bruises all along her neck. If it wasn't for her chest rising and falling, I'd think… I can't even think it. Her eyes flutter, giving me hope. "Baby, wake up."

Knowing I'm wasting precious time, I dial 9-1-1 as I pull her head onto my lap and brush away the hair that's stuck to her forehead and matted down by blood.

"9-1-1, what's your emergency?" a deep, male voice answers the line.

"Yes, my girlfriend was attacked and is unconscious. We're at the high school football game. Out at the end of the parking lot by the trees," I rush out and then pant to catch my breath.

"Okay, sir. Please take a deep breath. You're no good to her if you're not calm." He says the words as if he's said them a thousand times, which he probably has.

I take his advice and take as calming a breath as I can with the love of my life lying in my arms unconscious and beaten badly.

"Okay, I'm better now," I tell him.

"Good, now is she breathing? Does she have a pulse?"

"Yes, but she won't wake up."

"That's okay. I've got an ambulance en route to you as we speak. They should be there in two minutes. Is there anything else you can tell me?"

"Um… she's eight, almost nine months pregnant." Placing my hand over her stomach, I wait to see if I can feel the baby move. She's normally active this time of night, but as I wait, I don't feel any movement. "Is the baby okay?"

"I can't say, but the hospital will check both of them out."

"I can't lose her. I only just got her," I plead with the unknown man on the other end of the line.

"I understand and the EMTs will do everything in their power to help both of them. Is there someone there for you?"

"At the game, but not with me," I answer, smoothing my hand over Delilah's dark hair.

"I think you should have someone drive you to the hospital."

"Why?"

"You seem a little shaken up," he says.

"No shit, I'm shaken up. I can't wake her up and there might be something wrong with my baby," I growl, pulling the phone away and looking down at it before I hang up.

I see the lights at the same moment I hear my dad call out my name. I look around, but don't see him at first. He's weaving in and out of the cars, his gaze set on us.

The ambulance pulls up as close as the parking lot will allow before they hop out.

Everything after that happens in a blur. One moment I have Delilah in my arms, and the next she's being placed on a gurney and wheeled into the back of the ambulance.

My dad is talking, but I can't hear him. I don't hear anything. My entire focus is on Delilah's battered frame. The second the doors close, everything comes rushing back in. The sounds from the game, my dad talking with my mom, and November standing off to the side crying.

I'm rooted to my spot until I can no longer see the flashing lights.

Heading to my truck, I'm fumbling with my keys when I'm stopped by two hands gripping my shoulders. I swing around, ready to fight, needing to get to Delilah to make sure she's going to be okay. I stop when I see my dad standing there with worry creased across his face.

"Max, let me drive you. Asher and November are going to take Beckham to their house for the night. They've already said he can stay as long as you need. November's calling Ryder and Lexie to let them know what's happening and will keep me updated on them."

"Yeah, okay. Whatever, but I need to get to the hospital." I hit the key fob and wait for the doors to unlock, but nothing happens. "What's wrong with this fucking thing?" I growl and hit the button over and over again, expecting a different result. "Goddammit," I shout, kicking the tire.

It's then I see a set of keys on the ground with a big letter D on it by her purse. Bending down, I pick up Delilah's set of keys. "She was here. Trying to get into the truck." I hit the unlock button, but it doesn't work. "She couldn't get in."

"Max, forget about the truck for now. We can take mine. I'll have someone come get your truck later. It's not worth the worry." He starts to guide me in the opposite direction of the stadium.

Gripping my hair, I nearly tear it from the roots. "But it

is. If my damn truck would've unlocked maybe she could have gotten away."

He nods, walking me around his truck, and waits until I'm inside before he speaks. "I know things look bleak right now, but trust me, God did not bring that woman into your life to have her taken away. You have to believe everything will be okay."

"I don't know what I'll do if something happens to her or the baby. If she makes it through but loses the baby, she'll…" I choke on the words, unable to say them out loud. "I should have asked her to marry me. What was I waiting for?"

"The perfect moment, Son, and you'll get that moment. But right now, let's get to the hospital. What do you say?"

I nod, feeling numb.

Peeling out of the parking lot, my dad breaks every traffic law trying to get us to the hospital as quickly as possible. I stare out the windshield as I watch our town pass by. "Does Beck know?"

"Nothing yet, but Asher and November won't let him worry. He thinks he's having a sleepover with some of his cousins."

Cousins.

I needed to make it official.

As soon as I can.

Because Beck and Delilah deserve a big family.

The truck hasn't even stopped before I throw open my door and run through the emergency room's doors. I stop in front of a woman who looks like she's had a long day and knows I'm going to cause her problems going by the deep frown on her face.

"My girlfriend, Delilah Williams, was brought in not long ago. I found her unconscious and unresponsive. What room is she in?"

"I'm sorry, sir, but unless you're family I can't give you that information." She looks down and starts typing.

"I am family. She's having my baby." That should count for something, right?

"Who's to say you're not the one who put her in the hospital in the first place? I'm sorry, sir."

"I have to see her. I need to be there when she wakes up," I beg. I've always been calm, but in this moment, I feel like I'm close to losing my mind.

"Until she wakes up and says she wants to see you, you'll have to wait out here. Now, if you don't mind, there are others waiting."

I turn to find two other people waiting for help.

"What if her parents call and give their consent?" I bargain.

"I'm sorry, sir, unless they are present, I'd have no way of knowing if whoever calls is indeed her mother or father, or not. You could have anyone call and say they're her parents."

Fuck.

While I understand their need to keep patients safe, they don't need to keep her safe from me.

The fight goes out in me. "Can you let the doctors know I'm here for her?"

"Yes, I'll let them know." She looks behind me and calls out, "Next."

I find an empty seat close to the doors where I know someone will come out to give information and sit. I don't plan to move until I know how Delilah's doing.

It doesn't take long for my dad to find me. He silently sits beside me. My legs bounce as each minute seems like hours. Each time the doors swing open, I stand ready for news and each time it's for some other unlucky soul sitting in the emergency room waiting with us.

Every second feels like hours. My emotions are ping-ponging inside me going from despair to anger to guilt. I should have gone with her. If I'd been by her side, nothing would have happened.

My dad holds his phone out for me to read a text that just came in from Mom. Delilah's parents along with Ava are getting on the first available flight and will be here tomorrow.

"Thanks. I wish they were here now, so they could get us answers." I pull out my phone to see a dozen messages and missed calls, but don't bother to read them. What I do see is we've been here for well over an hour without an update. "What's taking so long?"

"I can't say, Son, but she's in good hands."

"What if it's the baby? I tried to feel if there was any movement and felt none. What does that mean?"

"It could mean a number of things." He claps me on the back and digs his fingers into my tense shoulder muscles. "Perhaps the baby was sleeping."

I hear what he doesn't say, though. Maybe the baby wasn't moving because she's hurt or worse.

"When I see her, I'm asking her to marry me. I can't wait any longer. I'm done giving her time."

"Maybe asking her first thing isn't the smartest thing, Son. She'll likely be out of it, and if not then in pain. Wait until she's safe at home."

"You think she'll say no?" I couldn't bear the possibility.

"Not on a normal day, but after today and whatever else she's gone through, we don't know what's possible. Feel out the situation before you storm in there and demand marriage."

"I wouldn't demand it. I'd do it proper," I bite out.

"Would you? Did you plan on asking with her in a hospital bed after being attacked?" I shake my head because he's right. "No, you didn't, so you're going to wait, and then she'll say yes."

"What if she doesn't pull through? I've never seen anyone as messed up as she is." Deep down, I know it was Stanton. What if he keeps coming back until he gets the job done?

"She's strong." He moves to squat down in front of me and locks eyes with me. "I know it's hard while we sit here waiting, but you have to believe in how strong she is."

"Is this what being in love is like? Always fearing the worst is going to happen?"

"Somedays, but for the most part, it's spending your life with the person you love most in the world. Your best friend, lover, and confidant. It's having someone there to share all of your good moments with, but also your bad."

"I want to be in there for her," I say hoarsely.

"I know you do, Son, and you will be. You said she was unconscious, so she doesn't know if you're there or not."

I know he's right, but that still doesn't make it any easier.

"When I tried to get back there, I told them the baby is mine," I confess, making sure no one overhears.

"She is yours. She may not have your blood, but that little girl will always be yours, blood or not."

The door swings open, and this time I don't have it in me to stand. A woman in scrubs looks around the room as she takes off her mask. "Mr. Black?"

"Here," I jump up and rush the short distance to her.

"I wanted to inform you that your daughter has been born. Right now, she's in the PICU being checked out. As soon as you can visit her, someone will be out to bring you back."

My daughter.

"It's too early," I argue.

"It is, but she's breathing on her own. Like I said, someone will be out to get you as soon as you can meet her."

"What about Delilah? Is she okay? We've had no word on her."

"As you know, she was badly beaten up. One of the complications was the placental abruption, and we had to perform a cesarean. Ms. Williams is in recovery and once she's awake and asking to see you, you can see her."

"Is she going to be okay?"

The nurse looks around and then leans in to speak quietly. "I'm not supposed to give you any information, but I can tell you this. She's going to be sore after the c-section and the bruises. There are a couple of fractured ribs that will make moving around more difficult, but give her some time and she'll be fine." She moves back a step "I need to get back in there. It's a busy night. It must be a full moon or something."

"Thank you, doctor. I appreciate it more than you'll ever know." My body sags with relief and now I feel drained.

"You're a father." My dad pats me on the back. "How does it feel?"

"Exhausting." I chuckle humorlessly. "I missed her birth. She'll always know I wasn't there."

"But you can tell her how much you wished you were. That you were right outside the doors. She doesn't need to know the rest. At least not for a long, long time. I'm going to step outside to call your mom and tell her the good news."

All I can do is sit down and nod. My mind is whirling with the news. We haven't even decided on a name yet. We thought we had time. We should have stayed home and then none of this would have happened.

Pulling my phone out, I dial her dad's number. He answers on the first ring. "Hello? Max?"

"Hey, I just wanted to let you know a doctor came out said they had to perform a c-section so the baby's here. She's in the PICU and Delilah's in recovery."

"Have you seen either one of them yet?"

"Not yet. She made it sound as if I'll get to see the baby first. I don't know if Delilah ever woke up. When I found her, she was—"

"She's going to pull through. She has to," Ryder chokes out.

"The doctor made it sound like she would, but until I see her awake with my own two eyes, I won't stop worrying."

"Call me after you see her and keep me updated. We won't be there until around eleven tomorrow morning."

He sounds just as worried as I am. I've been a father for all of two minutes and I already can't imagine how it would feel to be thousands of miles away from my little girl knowing she's hurt and there's nothing I can do about it.

"Beck is staying with November and Asher with some of the other kids. He doesn't know what's happening. Should I tell him?" I don't want him not to trust me after this.

"Not yet. Let him have tonight."

Yeah, tonight. Tomorrow he'll see his mom and know there really are monsters in the world.

"I'll call you when I know something more," I tell him, and then hang up.

Leaning back in my chair, I stretch my legs out, close my eyes, and wait.

When I open my eyes again, it will either be a new beginning with my family or the worst/best day of my life.

TWENTY-ONE
DELILAH

CONFUSED, I blink, or at least I think I'm blinking except when I try to open my eyes, I'm only met with blackness. I try to wipe at my eyes, but my arms are too heavy to lift.

I want to sit up and figure out where I am, but pain and something else altogether keeps me down. My entire body feels like it's being held down by a lead weight and my head is foggy. I can't remember where I am or what I was last doing.

Where am I?

"I think she's waking up," a familiar voice says.

Dad?

I try to turn my head toward the sound, but it's like I'm under water and can't come to the surface.

"Beauty?" Max questions, and there's a squeeze of my hand.

My fingers spasm in his hold, or at least I think they do.

"Open your eyes, beauty." There's a strange warble in his voice that has me doing everything I can to open my eyes to no avail.

A hand smooths over my forehead. "Take your time, sweetie. I know it's hard."

"Fight, baby girl," my dad chokes out.

I try. I don't want my loved ones to worry about me. I want to wake up and tell them everything is going to be okay, but instead, blackness wins out.

I wake up the same way over and over again. I have no idea how much time passes between each episode. Each time I try to move and try to open my eyes, but I'm unsuccessful so many times I don't know if I'll ever break out of this in between.

The next time I wake up, something feels different. I'm still in pain, but now it's more localized. My face and stomach throb. Tears sting the backs of my eyes and then I feel wetness trail down my cheek.

"Delilah, come back to us. We need you. Your daughter needs you." My mom's voice is close but far away at the same time.

My daughter?

Why would she need me?

Bradley.

I remember.

He found me and dragged me into the trees.

My face.

My stomach.

My baby.

What happened to my baby?

My hand makes jerking movements until it's covering the area of my torso that throbs.

I don't know what happened, but I can feel the difference. My baby's gone.

After what feels like forever, my eyes finally blink open. The world is blurry, but each time I blink it becomes more focused.

First, I see my mom's blue hair. There's no denying her blue shade. She's leaning against someone. My dad. I blink again and see the worry lines around his eyes and the way he's holding my mom together.

"Mom? Dad?" I rasp out.

Blinking again, I see their heads pop up before they lean close and take my hand in theirs.

"Baby girl," my dad sighs out. "You've had us so worried."

I tug at their hands and place them lightly over my deflated stomach. "Where's my baby?"

My dad brings our hands up to his mouth and kisses my knuckles. "She's fine. She's in the PICU waiting to meet her mom."

I watch as my mom hits the red button on my bed. A

moment later a voice calls out into the room. "Yes," a stern, but feminine voice rings out.

"My daughter's awake and talking." She says this as if I've been awake before but didn't speak.

"Okay, I'll inform the doctor and he'll be in soon."

"Where's Beck?" He was at the game. He must be so scared.

"He's with my mom and dad," I hear a rumble from beside me.

Turning my head carefully, I see Max sitting on the other side of the bed. He has dark slashes under his eyes that make it look like he hasn't slept in days.

"Max," I rasp out. I lift my hand, wanting to touch his face, but the tubes in my hand tug when I move, so I stop. "Come closer."

He leans in, but it's not enough.

"Why won't you move closer?" I whisper, wanting to feel the scruff on his face.

"I'm afraid I'll hurt you." His fingers twitch over mine.

"I want to touch your face. You look so…" I don't want to tell him how worried and bad he looks when I have no idea how long I've been here.

"You can say bad. Awful, even. I haven't slept in two days. Neither have your parents. We've been so worried about you. The doctors couldn't explain why you wouldn't wake up."

"I've been here for two days?" I ask as I try to sit up. But there's a sharp pain on one side along with my whole stomach. I'm weak and it feels like my stomach has no muscles to use. No matter how hard I try there's nothing but pain.

Mom stands and pushes me down gently. "No, no, no, honey. Lay back. You have to take it easy."

"What's wrong with me?" I look at each of them, waiting for them to tell me the damage Bradley inflicted upon me.

"They had to deliver the baby by c-section, but like your mother said, she's fine." My dad smiles at me and brushes his fingers along my hairline. "You're pretty banged up. You have two fractured ribs and lots of bruises, but they'll all heal in time."

A doctor and a nurse come in ushering everyone from the room so they can check me out. I answer all their questions, but my sole focus is on when I can see my daughter. It's my one and only goal.

"Have you seen her?" I look from my parents to Max once they're back in the room and sitting around the bed. "Is she beautiful?"

"Max thought you should see her first, and we tried to wait, but you were asleep for so long." My dad's eyes turn glassy for a moment before he rests his forehead on my hand.

My mom runs her fingers through his hair. "We didn't know how long you'd be asleep, and I knew you wouldn't want her to be alone for so long."

No, I don't want my baby girl to be alone. Not even for a minute. I want her to feel loved from the moment she was born. I hate that I couldn't be there with her, but I'm grateful they were.

"She looks just like you did when you were born. She's perfect." She reaches out to touch my face, but stops. Her chin quivers. "Are you in much pain?" She looks to my dad. "Where is the nurse with her pain meds?"

"It hurts, but I'll live. I want to see my baby." I'll give up all the drugs in the world that will make my pain go away if it means I can meet my daughter.

"The nurse should be here soon. She'll make you feel better and then you can meet your daughter," my dad says in a soothing voice.

"Did you decide on a name yet?" my mom asks with hope in her voice.

My poor baby's been here for two long days without a name.

I start to shake my head but stop when all it does is make my head hurt more.

"Can I have some water?" I ask, my voice still rough from misuse.

"Of course, sweetheart. I should have asked you first thing." She pours me some water and holds the cup with a straw in it up to my waiting mouth.

I take long draws, relishing the way the cool water feels

against my parched throat. When I come up for air, I find everyone looking at me. "I guess I was thirsty." I look to Max, who already looks lighter than he did when I first saw him. "I thought I had more time to name her. It hasn't been that long since we found out for sure we're having a girl."

Max cracks a small smile, but it doesn't meet his eyes. "She definitely wasn't cooperating on that front."

"Surely you must have had some names you like," Mom urges.

"I do, but I also thought I'd know when I saw her. Never did I think she'd be born with these circumstances." Emotion clogs my throat as tears well up and track down my cheeks. "She probably thinks I've abandoned her."

"No, baby girl." My dad stands and moves to stand up by my head. He brushes my hair from my face and dries my tears. "She doesn't think that. You know I wasn't there when you were born, right? I was on a plane and devastated I missed your birth, but you know what?" I barely give a shake to my head because I don't know. "You didn't care or know I wasn't there."

"I still loved you." My lower lip trembles. "But you understand how I feel."

Leaning down, he kisses my forehead. "I do, but don't let it ruin your first meeting with her. She's going to love you just as you love her."

A smiling nurse different from before comes in with a wheelchair. "Let's get you set up here," she says as she changes out one of my IV bags. "Now hit the button here and we'll give it a few minutes to work before we get you out of bed. Are the new parents excited to meet their baby?" she asks while checking my stats.

"Yes," I answer and look to Max.

He gives me a weak smile. "I wanted to see her for the first time with you."

"Come here," I beckon him. This time he listens, and when he's close enough, I lift my hands and pull him the rest of the way, so I can brush my mouth to his. I'm sure my breath is atrocious, so I don't take it any further.

Hovering over me, he speaks so only I can hear. "I told them I'm the father. I thought it would get me back to see you, but they wouldn't let me past the waiting room door."

Cupping one side of his face, I try to keep my voice steady as I speak. The number of emotions I'm feeling is overwhelming. "You are the father, Max. I hate that you waited but thank you. Let's go see our daughter. Together."

His eyes turn glassy as he nods. When his phone starts to ring, a look of annoyance crosses his face. He pulls his phone out and looks down at it. "Give me a minute, I need to answer this."

I watch as he walks out of the room with his phone to his ear and then turns to my parents.

"He's been so worried about you, baby girl." My dad rubs my leg through the blanket.

"He loves you so much," my mom says with a watery smile. "I'm glad you have him in your life."

"Me too, Mom. Me too."

It's only a couple of minutes later when Max walks in with a beaming smile. All the worry is gone from his face and he looks like my happy Max.

"That was Cobi. They caught Bradley. Cobi said he'll be by later to take your statement since they'll need it to formally charge Stanton. They found evidence in his SUV that might bring down the rest of his family."

"I won't be safe until they're all behind bars. If they know I'm the reason they arrested him, they'll come after me. They won't care if I just had a baby. In fact, they'll probably think it will make it easier to get me out of the picture."

"Don't worry. You won't be left alone until you're safe," Max grips my hand. "I'm not letting you out of my sight for a long time to come."

"I guess it's a good thing I like you then."

"I guess so." He winks.

The nurse who was in here earlier comes in with determination on her face. "Your meds should have kicked in by now, so let's get you up and out of bed."

While the pain has faded, I know it's going to hurt getting up and I'm dreading it.

Standing at the side of my bed, she encourages me to move. "The first time will be the hardest and after that, you'll know what you have to do to get yourself upright."

Gritting my teeth, I swear I almost crack a tooth as I try to eventually sit up. It's worse than I imagined, but now that I'm out of bed, I know I won't have to get back in for a while.

"When will I be discharged?"

The nurse chuckles. "Out of bed once and you're ready to get out of here."

It's true. I don't like staying in hospitals and I know I'll get next to no sleep while I'm here.

"You know where the PICU is?" she asks Max with hearts in her eyes.

I narrow them at her, but no one seems to notice. At least I don't think they do until I look over to my parents and they have cheesy grins on their faces.

Max comes to stand behind me, ready to wheel me to meet our daughter. "Yeah, I know the way."

"Now that you're awake, I think we'll go pick up Beck and take him home with us." My dad stands and helps my mom up. "If that's okay with you?"

"Maybe you can have him FaceTime me later." I want to see my boy.

"How about a phone call?" My mom suggests. "I think if he sees you beat up, he'll be more worried than he already is."

While I hate that she's right. I don't want to put any more undue stress on him. He's been through enough and I know it would better to see me in person like this rather than over the phone.

"Your right but call me so I can talk to him."

"I will, sweetie. Don't worry. Do you need anything, Max?" she asks.

"I'm good. I might run home to grab a shower and some things for Delilah and then come back."

"Make sure to eat. You've barely eaten anything," she tells him like she's his mom. It's strange having my parents like the man I'm with.

"I will," he tells her and gives her a small smile.

After both my parents kiss me goodbye, Max leads the way down a couple of long corridors until we're outside the pediatric intensive care unit. He pushes a button and once he tells them who we are, we're given the all clear to come in. We put on robes and masks and then scrub our hands.

It feels like forever before a nurse guides us through the area to where our baby's incubator stands.

"How long does she have to stay in there?" I ask as we near.

"She's actually being transferred to the nursery later today or she can be brought back to your room." The nurse turns back to look at us. "That's what's preferred."

"We can bring her back. I don't want to let her out of my sight after not being here for her the last two days." Max places his hand on my shoulder and squeezes it.

"Perfect. I'll let you meet your daughter and when you're ready to head back, we'll do the appropriate paperwork."

"Thank you." Placing my hand over Max's, I smile back at him. "Are you ready to finally meet her?"

"As ready as I'll ever be." He looks ahead and with each passing second his smile grows. "I guess it's a good thing we got the room ready extra early, huh?"

My mom spurred on the nursery by buying and shipping an entire furniture set after learning her newest grandchild was going to be a girl. Once it arrived, we set up the room with everything a baby could ever want.

"Now, I'm glad the room's ready for her. I don't think I'm fit enough right now to do much of anything."

"I wouldn't let you even if you tried. Now turn around and look who's in front of you."

I turn, not realizing we'd stopped. The nurse already has her out and is placing her in my arms. Right in that moment, all is right with the world.

The second I see her, I know her name.

Luna.

She shines as bright as the full moon on a clear night.

She's absolutely perfect.

Her hair is so light it's almost translucent. I can tell she's going to be blonde just like me and her brother. My eyes flick up to Max. Even just like her dad.

"She's perfect," Max says in awe.

"Her name's Luna."

"I think you're right. She was born with the full moon high in the sky. Luna Black. It's fitting." Squatting down beside me, he runs one long finger over her peach fuzz hair and down her cheek.

Leaning down, I kiss her forehead and breath in her sweet baby scent. "I love you, Luna."

EPILOGUE
MAX

3 Months Later

WE ALL SIT TRANSFIXED as a special new bulletin breaks across the bottom of the screen of the World Series.

All three Stanton's are now being held after further investigation into evidence that was found when Bradley Stanton attacked his ex-girlfriend in Murfreesboro, Tennessee, three months ago. She'd been in hiding after learning he ran a drug and human trafficking ring, forcing the women to sell drugs for his family. Since then, evidence has come to light that more than ten women were killed by one of the three Stantons' hands.

I look to find Delilah nowhere in the room and realize she's been gone for quite some time now. It brings back a sense of deja vu that I don't like. I can't stand to have her out of sight for too long after what happened to her the night of the football game. The night she was beaten. The night our daughter was born.

"I'll be back," I announce as I leave the room.

Delilah's parents and sister look at me with worry in their eyes, but the rest of the room can't take their eyes off the TV and the breaking news.

Heading upstairs, I find the bathroom door in the master suite closed.

"Beauty?" I call as I knock on the door and open it. I'm shocked to find Delilah sitting on the floor with tears trailing down her cheeks. I move to sit beside her and then pull her into my lap. "Hey, what's wrong?"

Burying her face in my chest, I can feel her tears through my shirt as she continues to cry.

"I got worried when you were gone for so long."

"I'm sorry," she squeaks out.

"Do you want me to get your mom up here?" She shakes her head. "Ava?" I question, but she shakes her head no again. "Your dad?"

Delilah gets on her knees, straddling my legs, and hugs my neck. "I only want you."

"Well, you've got me. On the bathroom floor and all. It's a good thing I splurged for the heated floors." I chuckle and kiss the side of her head. "Tell me what's wrong, beauty. I can't help if I don't know what's got you crying."

"You know how I've been feeling extra tired and a little sick this week?" she asks through her sniffles.

"Yes, but that's normal. We've got a newborn who wants to eat every two hours. With Beck going back to school and you insisting on getting up in the mornings with him, you've been running yourself ragged. Plus, there's that bug going around."

"It's not just that." She shifts on my lap and holds out a white stick. "I'm pregnant."

Words fail me. It's not that I don't believe her, but we didn't think it was possible for Delilah to get pregnant with her breastfeeding. We've talked about having another child someday, but not this soon. She wanted to wait at least a year or two.

Is she regretting she's pregnant?

Settling on my lap, her glassy blue eyes take me in. "I'm the poster child for unplanned pregnancies. Is it too much to ask for me to be married just once?" she cries.

"Is that what this is about? You want to be married before the baby comes." If that's the case, I'll drag her ass to the courthouse tomorrow and marry her.

"It would be nice," she huffs. "How am I going to have two babies? I'm never going to sleep again."

"Beauty, that's what I'm here for. I'll help you in any way I can. I'll get up in the middle of the night and do feedings and change diapers. Whatever you want from me, I'll do it."

Resting her forehead to mine, she nods. "You'd do all that and more, I know it."

"I would," I agree.

"At least this time, I'm in love with the father of my baby."

"That's good to hear." I kiss her nose and then each corner of her mouth. "Since we're sharing good news here, I came to find you to tell you that Stanton the first and second are now both in jail right along with the third. You don't have to worry about them any longer. You're free."

Her eyes widen, and a beautiful smile breaks out on her tear-streaked face. "Really?"

"Really." My hands move underneath her skirt to find her without panties and cup her ass. "I think we should celebrate."

"What about everyone downstairs? Won't they wonder where we are?" she asks even though she's pulling her shirt over her head. Leaving her lush and full breasts on display for me. Dipping my head, I take one pink nipple into my mouth over the lace of her bra. My tongue swirls around the fabric, making her moan.

"Do you really care about them right now?"

Not wasting any time, I raise my hips and pull my jeans down to my knees and let my cock spring free. Delilah's warm hands wrap around my length and starts to stroke.

"Ride me," I groan on the down stroke. "Later, once we have more time, I'll eat that sweet pussy of yours."

Getting up on her knees, she positions herself until she's got my cock at her opening and then she slowly starts to slide her way down. Her pussy is like heaven, and it's all mine.

"Oh god, you feel so good," she moans, full of me, and starts to rock her hips.

Cupping her tits, I kiss along her jaw and the column of her neck. Moving back up, I nip at her earlobe. I feel her walls start to flutter around me. I love how responsive she is and how easily she is to make come.

"I need more. Please, Max, I need to come now."

Never one to deny her, I run my hand down between us and gather up her juices to rub slow circles on her clit with my thumb. Wanting to come with her, I piston my hips up increasing our speed. We turn frantic on the bathroom floor not caring how loud we are or about the people who are downstairs. With Delilah in my arms, she shudders and moans her release into my neck. It's only moments later I surge up and let loose inside of her. Coating her inside with my seed.

Pride swells up in me knowing Delilah loves me, I impregnated her against the odds, and I'll get to see her round with child again.

Lifting her head, Delilah looks up at me with sleepy, sated eyes. "I think you just claimed me."

"Fuck, yes, I did. And tomorrow, if you want, I'll take you down to the courthouse and claim you all over again."

"I like the sound of that, but maybe we can do something small here with our family before the weather turns bad. That's if you're proposing to me."

Tipping my head back, I laugh. Never did I dream I'd propose marriage on the bathroom floor, but here I am doing just that. "Delilah Williams, would you do me the great honor of becoming Mrs. Max Black?"

"Yes," she cries with tears of joy in her eyes. "Oh god, I'm going to be a mess of emotions." She laughs. "Are you sure you want to marry me?"

"I've never been more sure about anything in my life." Standing with her in my arms, I set her on her feet and right her skirt. "Now let's get cleaned up and go downstairs to tell everyone the good news."

Read Ryder and Lexie's story in THE MODEL.

AFTERWORD

Have you checked out the other amazing stories in the Happily Ever Alpha World? Click on the link to continue reading another Happily Ever Alpha Book -> Aurora Rose Reynolds's Happily Ever Alpha World

About Boom Factory Publishing

Aurora Rose Reynolds and her husband, Sedaka Reynolds, created Boom Factory Publishing to use their experiences to expand and promote upcoming and existing indie authors.

With over six years in the industry, and millions of books sold worldwide, we know what it takes to become a successful author and we will use this knowledge to take our authors to the next level.

"As a successful hybrid author in this ever evolving industry, I know that you're only as successful as the team that is promoting you!" – Aurora Rose Reynolds

Please check out Boom Factory Publishing's website to see all of our talented authors and the books they have published.

https://boomfactorypublishing.com/

Don't miss out on any exciting news from Boom Factory Publishing! Subscribe to our newsletter at by clicking HERE.

Did you enjoy UNTIL DELILAH? If so, please consider leaving a review on Goodreads, Amazon, or BookBub. Reviews mean the world to authors especially to authors who are starting out. You can help get your favorite books into the hands of new readers.

I'd appreciate your help in spreading the word and it will only take a moment to leave a quick review. It can be as short or as long as you like. Your review could be the deciding factor or whether or not someone else buys my book.

To stay up to date on all my releases subscribe to my newsletter. https://harlowlayne.com/newsletter/

ACKNOWLEDGMENTS

My family- your support means so much. Thank you for all of your encouragement and giving me the time to do what makes me happy.

Aurora Rose Reynolds, Jessica Marin and Boom Factory Publishing: Thank you for giving me the opportunity to write in this wonderful world.

Wendy and Amanda: Thank you for reading my words before they're ready for eyes to see them. Thank you for your feedback and loving Max and Delilah.

Kelsey and Carmel: If it wasn't for our online writing, I'm not sure how many books I'd get done. Thank you for always being there. Thank you CJ for giving Beck's polar bear a name when my mind went blank.

Thank you **Kristen Breanne** for making my story into a book.

To all my **author friends**, you know who you are. Thank you for accepting me and making me feel welcome in this amazing community.

To **Give Me Books**, thank you for all your knowledge and for helping me make Until Delilah a success!

Lovers thank you for always being there.

Team Harlow's Girls: Each and everyone of you are amazing. Thank you for all of your support. You ROCK!

To each and every **reader**, **reviewer**, and **blogger** - I would be nowhere without you. Thank you for taking a chance on an unknown author.

ABOUT HARLOW

Harlow Layne is a hopeless romantic who is known for her contemporary writing style of beautiful slow-burn, sweet, sexy and swoon-worthy alpha and fast pace, super steamy romance in her Love is Blind series.

When Harlow's not writing you'll find her online shopping on Amazon, Facebook, or Instagram, reading, or hanging out with her family and two dogs.

Indie Author. Romance Writer. Reader. Mom. Wife. Dog Lover. Addicted to all things Happily Ever After and Amazon.

ALSO BY HARLOW LAYNE

Fairlane Series - Small Town Romance

With Love, Alex - Women's Fiction, Self Discovery

Hollywood Redemption - Single Parent, Suspense

Unsteady in Love - Second Chance, Military

Kiss Me - Holiday, Insta-Love

Fearless to Love - Insta- Love

Love is Blind Series- Reverse Age Gap Romance

Intern - Office Romance

The Model - Workplace Romance

The Bosun - Military, First Responder

The Doctor - Raine's story - October 14

The Rocker - Coming February 17, 2022

Hidden Oasis Series

Walk the Line - First Responder, Suspense

Secret Admirer - Damsel in Distress, Opposites Attract, Suspense

Til Death Do Us Part - Accidental Marriage, Insta-love

MM Romances

You Make It Easy -Second Chance

My Ex Girlfriend's Brother - MM - November 8

Chance Encounter - Enemies-to-Lovers - December 10

Collaborations

Basic Chemistry - Student/Teacher - Sept 2, 2021

Forever - Student/Teacher, Curvy girl, enemies-to-lovers - October 8, 2021

Worlds

Cocky Suit - RomCom, Office, Interracial

Risk - Forbidden, Sports

Affinity - Part of the Fairlane Series - Accidental Marriage, Enemies-to-Lovers

Until Delilah - Single Parent, Romantic Suspense with The Model tie-in

Printed by BoD"in Norderstedt, Germany